SPECIAL MESSAGE TO READERS

THE ULVERSCROFT FOUNDATION
(registered UK charity number 264873)

was established in 1972 to provide funds for
research, diagnosis and treatment of eye diseases.
Examples of major projects funded by
the Ulverscroft Foundation are:-

- The Children's Eye Unit at Moorfields Eye Hospital, London
- The Ulverscroft Children's Eye Unit at Great Ormond Street Hospital for Sick Children
- Funding research into eye diseases and treatment at the Department of Ophthalmology, University of Leicester
- The Ulverscroft Vision Research Group, Institute of Child Health
- Twin operating theatres at the Western Ophthalmic Hospital, London
- The Chair of Ophthalmology at the Royal Australian College of Ophthalmologists

You can help further the work of the Foundation
by making a donation or leaving a legacy.
Every contribution is gratefully received. If you
would like to help support the Foundation or
require further information, please contact:

THE ULVERSCROFT FOUNDATION
The Green, Bradgate Road, Anstey
Leicester LE7 7FU, England
Tel: (0116) 236 4325

website: www.foundation.ulverscroft.com

THE LOCKET OF
LOGAN HALL

Newly widowed Emily believes she will never love again. Working as an assistant in flirtatious Cameron's antiques shop, she finds a romantic keepsake in an old writing desk. Emily and Cameron set off on a hunt for the original owner, and the discoveries they make on the way change both of them forever. But Emily doesn't realise that Cameron is slowly falling in love with her. Is his love doomed to be unrequited, or will Emily see what's right in front of her — before it's too late?

Books by Christina Garbutt
in the Linford Romance Library:

MYSTERY AT MORWENNA BAY

CHRISTINA GARBUTT

THE LOCKET
OF LOGAN HALL

Complete and Unabridged

LINFORD
Leicester

First published in Great Britain in 2017

First Linford Edition
published 2019

*A catalogue record for this book is available
from the British Library.*

ISBN 978–1–4448–4326–2

Published by
F. A. Thorpe (Publishing)
Anstey, Leicestershire

Set by Words & Graphics Ltd.
Anstey, Leicestershire
Printed and bound in Great Britain by
T. J. International Ltd., Padstow, Cornwall

This book is printed on acid-free paper

1

Emily strolled along the promenade, the summer sun warming her back. In the distance Brighton Pier was still and calm. How lucky to have this beautiful walk into work. How many people could say the morning commute was one of their favourite times of the day? Not yet early enough for the tourists to be up and about and with the sea glistening like a jewel, it was Emily's own slice of paradise.

She waved to the girls setting up the ice cream kiosk and they grinned back. They were so young, as Emily had been when she'd spent a summer working there as a student, every day filling cone after cone with the soft white ice cream. The characters who visited the stall and the girls she'd worked with made the job so much fun. The smell of vanilla always brought back memories of the girl she'd been then, full of hope and excitement for the endless possibilities of life.

It was too early for ice cream but she promised herself she'd be back at lunchtime. Surely three whippies in a week wasn't too much?

Emily turned off the promenade and walked slowly up to McKenzie & Brown's, the second hand furniture shop she'd been working at for the last three weeks. The work was more interesting than she'd been anticipating, but she wouldn't be sad when she finished at the end of the summer — partly because the pay was pitiful and partly because of the shop's owner.

Mum had clearly been in full match-making mode when she'd arranged for Emily, much to Emily's surprise, to help Cameron out by working as his assistant. Her new boss was, without a shadow of a doubt, a very good-looking man. He was tall and dark and had a figure that suggested athletic free time. He also had buckets of charm, which made women young and old flock to him. Female customers rarely left without buying something after he'd wooed them into it.

Mum had obviously seen him as an ideal candidate to help Emily on her road to recovery — although she'd never admit it. He'd certainly turned on the charm in her first week but he must have realised his flirting was getting him nowhere because, mercifully, he'd stopped. This week their relationship had been purely professional, just as Emily liked it.

Emily arrived at the shop and used her key to let herself in. The inside was cool, as the morning sun had yet to reach the shop's windows. She stopped to look at her display of vases. When she'd started these had been randomly displayed on a shelf with no thought to their aesthetic appeal, so she had arranged them towards the front of the shop, filling some of them with flowers. If a few more sold this week they'd need to be restocked.

The rest of the shop needed the same attention. Furniture was jammed into every conceivable bit of floor space, so walking around to take a look at anything wasn't easy. If you made the effort then the furniture was lovely; Cameron clearly had a good eye when it came to purchasing stock — although not for layout.

Emily had been arranging the furniture in her head for a few days now and next time Cameron was out she was going to put her plan into action.

He wasn't around now but she could hear him moving about in his flat above the shop, so she went into the kitchenette to make a cup of tea.

He turned up, smelling of soap and with his dark brown hair still damp from the shower, as the kettle finished boiling.

'Tea?' she asked.

'Great, thanks. Listen, did you manage to finish the desk yesterday?'

Although the shop had several desks for sale she didn't need to ask which one he meant, since the big antique oak piece was the jewel in the shop's crown.

'Not yet. I'll get on it straight away.'

'Great.' And that was the end of their interaction for the morning — which was, she assured herself, much better than the flirting.

★ ★ ★

Slowly Emily eased the lid up on the writing desk. The musty smell of old wood wafted up and she inhaled deeply. How many women had sat at this desk writing letters? What intrigues had it seen in its two-hundred-year history?

Yesterday she'd cleaned the outside. She'd taken it slowly, wanting to spend as much time with this desk as possible because it piqued her imagination.

She pulled out the first letter drawer. It was in pristine condition. She gently wiped her soft cotton cloth around the wood and replaced it. The next drawer contained a dead spider, which disappointingly the most exciting thing she found in any of the tiny letter drawers. She'd been hoping for a notebook at the very least.

Emily pulled out a larger drawer and placed it on a protective sheet. She wiped over the inside and turned it over to do the base. As she did so she noticed it appeared to be larger on the outside than the inside. She ran her fingers around the edge; they were smooth. Lifting the drawer, she found a tiny keyhole on the back of the drawer. She'd found a secret compartment! Excitedly abandoning her cleaning, she pulled open the remaining drawers and cupboards, searching for a key. There was nothing but more dust.

'Coo-ee, only me,' called a voice from behind.

'Mum, what are you doing here?'

'I've come to take you for an early lunch.'

'It's only eleven-thirty.'

'Yes, as I said, it's an *early* lunch. Oh, would you look at that desk? It's gorgeous! See, I told you this would be an interesting job. When am I ever wrong? Well, there was the time with those peas but the less said about that the better. Now, let's tell Cameron we're going.'

Not waiting for an answer Maddie headed onto the shop floor.

Emily sighed and peeled off her cotton gloves. Searching for a key would have to wait. Mum was hard to argue with; kind, thoughtful and bossy, you knew she always had your best interests at heart — even if you didn't always agree with her.

By the time Emily joined her, Maddie was in deep conversation with Cameron. He'd already turned on the charm and watching them was to see a mutual appreciation club in progress.

'I'm halfway through the desk,' Emily said, interrupting their conversation. 'I'll finish it when I get back. It doesn't need a lot of work.'

'No worries. Enjoy your lunch.'

Cameron turned the full force of his devastating smile on Emily. A different woman's knees would have weakened. Emily felt nothing.

She nodded. 'See you later. Come on, Mum.'

Emily linked her arm through Maddie's and pulled her to the door. It was difficult because Maddie seemed intent on a prolonged goodbye to Emily's boss.

'Emily, how can you be so rude to Cameron?' she asked once they were finally out of the shop.

'I wasn't rude,' said Emily.

'A smile wouldn't have gone amiss.'

Emily dodged a family of tourists, who were intent on the sights and not on where they were headed. Maddie stumbled into her and the comforting scent of magnolia washed over Emily. She wasn't going to argue with the woman who loved her most.

'Let's eat here,' Emily said, ignoring her mum's comment while gently tugging her into a tiny café. 'They do great sandwiches.'

Emily went in search of a table while

Maddie queued for the lunch. She found a table wedged between a business man tapping frantically at his laptop and a boisterous family of five who were spilling out of their seats and talking over each other.

She hoped the overcrowded atmosphere would stop Maddie trying to instigate one of her heart-to-heart conversations.

'There you are, love, that'll fill you up. No, don't be silly, this is on me.'

Emily put her purse back in her handbag and picked up her baguette. She was starving and the thick, crunchy bread was just what she needed. Coronation chicken as well — her favourite.

'So Emily, about your rudeness to Cameron . . . ' Oh no, the packed room wasn't going to stop her! 'I think you should make an effort to be nicer to him, you know. You could get the job back when you return from your travels.'

'Mum, it's a low-paid job in a

second-hand furniture shop. I'm happy to do it for the summer but it's not something I want to do long term. Besides,' she said before taking another big bite, 'I wasn't rude to him.'

Maddie picked up her serviette and spread it neatly over her powder-blue linen skirt.

'Emily, you can't go shutting all men out just because of — '

'Mum,' said Emily, laying her hand over her mother's slender fingers, 'We've had this conversation so many times. I admit I've had some dark times over the last two years but I'm in a contented place now. I had Johnny and he's gone and I've accepted it. I don't need another man in my life.' Smiling slightly she added, 'I thought this job was to help Cameron out — not a ploy for me to end my single status.'

Maddie's ears turned pink. 'I'm not suggesting you marry him, darling! I'm just saying that showing him a bit of friendliness wouldn't be the end of the world.'

'OK, I promise I'll throw in a smile every now and then when I talk to him. Now, would you like some cake when you've finished the sandwich? They do a lovely carrot cake.'

'Let's share one. I need to watch my figure.' Maddie patted her stomach, which was as flat as when she'd been twenty.

Standing in the queue for the counter, Emily watched her mother finish her sandwich. She was a tiny woman, and with her shoulder-length blonde hair fading to grey she looked like an older version of Emily.

Emily was an only child and so Maddie had always been a big part of her life. When she'd implied she needed some help around the house now she was getting older, Emily hadn't hesitated to pack up her life in London and head home.

It had been a con, however. Emily's parents were as fit and as busy as ever. It was Emily that needed looking after — or so Maddie seemed to think! No sooner had she installed Emily back in her childhood bedroom than she told her she'd got her a job helping out her new neighbour's son.

Emily, in a fit of almost teenage rebellion even though she was fast approaching thirty, had told her mum she planned to use Johnny's insurance money to travel the world as soon as the summer ended. It wasn't true, of course.

She'd been content in her safe but dull life before and would have carried on living it indefinitely if her mother hadn't interfered. Emily was still working up the nerve to go into a travel agent — but she had to go through with the trip now, otherwise Maddie would start enrolling her on life enhancement courses while organising a parade of eligible bachelors!

Back at the shop, after a slight skirmish over the cake — she should have bought two as Maddie always ate more than she intended — Emily tentatively approached Cameron.

The shop was empty and he was sitting at the counter, head in his hands looking at a spreadsheet covered in numbers. It didn't take a genius to see the shop was struggling and by the look on Cameron's face there wasn't any sign of improvement.

'Hi,' she volunteered.

'Hey,' he said, looking up from the sheet.

'Were you given keys with the antique desk?'

He looked surprised. 'I don't think so. Why?'

'I've found what I think is a keyhole at the back of one of the drawers.'

'Really?' Cameron stood up and his papers slithered to the floor. 'Can you show me?'

Emily would have preferred to solve the puzzle by herself but as it was his shop after all, she couldn't stop him. She showed him the drawer and how it seemed to be larger on the outside.

He picked it up to examine it himself. After a moment he looked up and grinned at her.

'You're right, it's a secret compartment. I wonder if there's anything in it.' He gave the drawer a gentle shake. It made no sound.

'It's probably just full of dust,' she said.

'Yeah . . . But still, let's give the desk a thorough search. The key could be hidden in one of the other drawers or taped to the back of something.'

'I've cleaned each one, so . . . '

'Let's look anyway.'

They worked through the drawers together in silence but as Emily predicted they were all empty.

'Oh well,' said Cameron, 'it was worth a try.'

Emily said nothing, she was feeling absurdly disappointed.

'Unless . . . ' said Cameron as he opened a cupboard in the base of the desk. 'No, nothing in here.' He opened the other cupboard and stuck his head in. 'Ah,' he said triumphantly. 'Yes, I think that might be . . . hmmm . . . '

He pulled his head back out.

'I think there might be something in the corner at the back but my fingers are too big. Perhaps you could have a go?'

There was a small dent in the wood, just big enough for a finger tip. Emily prodded and pushed it in several directions but nothing happened.

'Nope. Any suggestions?' she called out.

'Try lifting it.'

Sure enough, a small section of wood lifted to reveal a rectangular indentation. Lying in the centre of that was a key.

'A key! I've found it!' she shrieked, promptly banging her head on the roof of the cupboard.

'Careful,' said Cameron. 'Let's see . . . Oh yeah, that's got to be the one.' Emily held it out to him. 'No I don't want it. You should be the one to open the compartment. You discovered it, after all.'

She put the key in the lock. It was a perfect fit.

'Now don't be disappointed if it's empty,' Cameron warned.

She turned the key. The drawer sprang open and they both peered forward.

Inside was an envelope stained brown with age . . .

2

Emily's eyes were sparkling with excitement, and it was the most life Cameron had seen in her since they'd met. Normally he felt it was like working with a robot — she was efficient, polite and hardworking but not exactly friendly.

When his father's next-door neighbour had suggested her widowed daughter as a solution to his staffing crisis Cameron expected a much older woman, so Emily was a shock. Beautiful in an elfin kind of way, with large green eyes and pale skin, he was immediately attracted to her. When she said she could only stay for the summer it was a no-brainer — they could have a little fun and then go their separate ways with no harm done on either side.

However, it was not to be as no amount of gentle teasing could break through the barriers she'd clearly erected around herself. Cameron wasn't going to try any harder. He liked his women as fun and anti-commitment as he was, and Emily was just too complicated.

Nevertheless, with her eyes sparkling and her cheeks flushed he could see the woman she had been before tragedy had struck.

'Shall we open it?' she said.

He laughed. 'Might as well.'

She went over to her cleaning supplies and slipped on some cotton gloves. She'd been watching too many TV dramas. The letter wasn't that old — somewhere between fifty and a hundred years, at a guess.

She gently removed it from the drawer and held it up so they both could see. There was no writing on the front of the envelope. She turned it over; either it had never been sealed or the glue had weakened with age as the flap was open.

'There's something small and hard in here.'

'Tip it out so we can see.'

She flipped the envelope over and gave it a gentle shake. Something fell onto her hand. Cameron lent closer to get a better look but noticed the stiffening of her shoulders so he stepped back.

'It's a locket,' she said, holding it up.

'See if it opens.'

Emily put the letter down and tried to open the tiny clasp but her fingers were too clumsy with the gloves on.

'Let me try.' Cameron went to take the locket from her but her fingers curled around it protectively. 'I don't think it's that delicate. Or that old. Maybe fifty to eighty years or so.'

He almost laughed at the disappointment on her face but managed to hold back. She wasn't the sort of woman you laughed at.

He took the locket, his fingers brushing her hand as he did so. He noticed she tensed again, which was irritating. After all, he wasn't about to pounce on her!

Inside the locket there was a black

and white photograph of a man in some kind of uniform but it was so faded it was difficult to make out any detail. He handed the locket back to Emily.

She stared at it for a moment and then placed it reverently on the desk. She picked up the envelope and said, 'There's paper in here as well. It could be a letter.'

There was excitement in her voice again.

She took the paper out giving it the same deference as if she'd found important lost scrolls.

'It is a letter. It says, *My darling Dottie, please keep this locket safe. Wear it close to your heart until I return to you. All my love, now and always, Harry.* It's dated March, 1940.'

Emily returned the letter to the envelope.

'That's beautiful,' she said.

'Not that beautiful. It's not as if Dottie did wear it close to her heart, is it? Otherwise, what's it doing stuffed in a secret drawer?'

Instantly, he knew he'd said the wrong thing. Any camaraderie they'd shared over the discovery, any barriers he thought might be coming down had gone right back up. He could see it in the stiffness of her shoulders and the way she turned away from him to pick up the locket.

'Right, well . . . ' he said. 'I'll take a look at the paperwork and see if we can get it returned to its rightful owner.'

'You'll do that?' she asked. Her voice was thick and when she turned to look at him he could see that her eyes were glistening with unshed tears. What on earth was wrong? What he'd said wasn't that bad! Talking to her was harder than negotiating a minefield.

'Of course,' he said. 'It should be a simple matter of going through the papertrail. Somewhere along its owner-ship we'll find a Harry or a Dottie.'

Backing away as quickly as he could from the potential tears, he made his way back into the shop, which was depressingly still empty of customers.

He'd been looking at his accounts when Emily had come back from lunch. The mystery of Dottie and her lover would have to wait; the number-crunching had to come first.

He picked up the spreadsheets sent over by his accountant and groaned. They made dire reading. When Peter had suggested they sell the business, he should have listened. Buying out his best friend had taken almost all of his money and the financial responsibility of looking after the business on his own was quickly becoming a nightmare. He was forced to admit that, while he was the best at finding furniture people would buy, Peter had been much better at the business end of things. Cameron was like a duck out of water; able to walk but not with much dignity.

One temporary solution kept presenting itself — he could rent out the flat attached to the shop and move back in with his father. It would give him an independent source of income coming in each month as well as some much-needed cash.

The only problem was moving back in with his father. Alastair was great fun, more like an older brother than a dad and he'd been great to grow up with, but now Cameron had left home his father was back on the dating scene with a vengeance and Cameron would cramp his style!

He took another look at the figures and sighed. It was time to call his father.

* * *

In the end Alastair made it easy for him. He didn't have to ask before his father offered the use of his spare room. Cameron hoped it would only be a temporary measure for both their sakes.

He called around some estate agents, all of whom were keen to get his flat on the market without even looking at it. The sums they suggested for rent went some way to easing his mind about his cash flow problems.

If Emily was ready to man the shop by herself by next week, he could visit a few house clearances and hopefully get in some good quality stock.

'Have you looked up those papers yet?'

Cameron jumped. He'd completely forgotten Emily was still in the shop.

'Erm, no . . . I'm afraid I haven't, not yet.'

'Do you want me to do it?'

Cameron didn't want Emily going through his paperwork. She might get a glimpse of how bad the business finances were and he didn't want anyone to know.

'It's all right. I'll do it now.'

He went through to his office and pulled open a filing cabinet. Anyone else would see a jumble of papers but he knew where everything was. Well, most of the time . . . He got lucky and pulled out the paperwork straight away.

'Here.' He handed it all over to Emily who didn't even sit down before starting to wade through it.

'It says here you picked up the desk from Whealdon Community Hall.'

'That's right, they were selling off furniture cheaply before demolishing the building. It was a shame really because the old building had such character, but with a dodgy roof and a bit of subsidence I guess it had to go.'

Emily surprised him by laughing.

'You're right, they should have kept it and when the ladies of the WI disappeared down a sink hole the community would have shrugged their shoulders and said, 'well at least we kept that building going a few more years'.' She pulled a sheet from the file. 'This paperwork says the desk was a donation to the council fifteen years ago but it doesn't give a name.' She rifled through the rest of the paperwork. 'There's nothing else here to show who it's from.'

'OK — well, I guess that's it then.'

Cameron glanced at his phone as it pinged. An email flashed up on his screen — an estate agent wanted to call round in just over an hour to take some photos of the flat. He needed to get a move on if it was going to be presentable.

'Unless . . . ' said Emily intruding on his thoughts, 'Unless we go to Logan Hall ourselves.'

'Where?'

'I took another look at the letter and it's on headed paper from somewhere called Logan Hall. I'm sure that will be easy enough to find. We could go and check it out.'

Was she insane? He didn't have the time, resources or inclination to go off on some wild goose chase!

'Look, it's all very romantic finding an old love letter but let's face it, it's highly unlikely the people involved are even still alive,' he pointed out reasonably.

'But they might be. Or at least one of them might be. We owe it to them.'

'We don't owe them anything. To be frank, I don't have the time or money to look into this right now.'

She looked as if she was about to protest.

'That's my final decision, Emily.'

3

Emily's hair whipped around her face, getting in her eyes and mouth, but she wasn't about to shut the car window. Without the strong breeze the car was like a greenhouse — but with the aroma of old sport socks rather than the soft scent of fresh tomatoes.

Cameron had explained that his air conditioning didn't work when she'd got into the car an hour ago. It was pretty much all he'd said since picking her up.

She glanced at her watch again. In about twenty minutes they'd be at Logan Hall.

Poor Cameron, he didn't want to be doing this on his day off but she'd struck a deal with him. She'd Googled Logan Hall and found it was close to Brighton, an hour and a half's drive at the most. It was open to the public so they'd be able to take a look around.

The trouble was, she didn't drive and so she needed Cameron to take her. But she'd seen the scepticism in his brown eyes and she knew he thought the whole thing was a waste of time.

After Googling Logan Hall she'd looked up McKenzie & Brown's website. It was out of the ark! The interface was clumsy and the stock showing was outdated. Her fingers itched to update it; the first time she'd felt any inclination to program for two years. Maddie would have taken it as a 'good sign' but anyone with programming experience would see it as a challenge — it was that bad.

So she offered to update it for free — if Cameron would take her to Logan Hall.

She could see he was unimpressed, even though it would save him a considerable sum of money as well as potentially helping sales. So she did what she'd always sworn not to do. She played the widow card.

'The thing is,' she'd said, 'if someone were to give me a letter from Johnny, now or in eighty years' time, it would mean so much to me. I just want the opportunity to do the same for these people.'

As soon as she mentioned Johnny, she could see that she had him. The widow card trumped his reluctance. She didn't feel bad. After all, he was getting a free overhaul of his website. He was going to get far more out of this than she was. Besides what she'd said was the truth — and it was exactly why she wanted to return the letter and the necklace to the owners.

Emily glanced across at Cameron. His long fingers on his right hand were tapping the steering wheel. His other hand rested on his thigh. He was frowning at the road, his gaze flicking from the window to the rear-view mirror and back. He'd not shaved this morning and Emily could see flecks of red and grey among the dark stubble.

She turned her attention back to the

road. A sign indicated that Logan Hall was on the left. Cameron turned into the driveway. Tall trees lined the way, their over hanging leaves creating a rippling soft green tunnel.

They turned a corner and Emily gasped. The house was beautiful with its soft yellow bricks covered in climbing roses. Wide steps led the way to the front door, which was framed by large windows on either side.

Cameron grunted next to her.

'It's very striking,' he said.

'What were you expecting?'

He shrugged, 'I'm not expecting anything. This is your treasure hunt.'

Emily grinned. She preferred him like this, grumpy and slightly belligerent. It felt more real than the charming persona he tended to put on for other people.

Cameron pulled into the car park. His was only the third car there.

'Looks like this is the place to be.'

Emily ignored his sarcasm and stepped out of the car. A cooling breeze gently lifted her hair. She stretched and smiled. This was the perfect setting for a love story. She strode off towards the entrance, not checking to see if Cameron was coming too.

She was halfway across the car park when she heard the car lock and the crunch of gravel as he followed her. By the time she pushed open the large oak front door he had caught up with her.

Emily stepped inside and was immediately disorientated by the darkness of the hallway. She blinked a few times before her surroundings came into focus. A tiny woman was beaming at them from behind a rickety desk, her gunmetal grey hair secured in a rigid perm.

'Hello,' she called. 'Welcome to Logan Hall. I'm Nana and if there's anything I can help you with, please let me know.'

She handed Cameron two laminated cards as Emily paid their entrance fee.

'A few rooms are closed today because of updating but you'll still get to see most of the house. Take this door to the left and follow the rooms round.

There's a gift shop and a tea room towards the end of the tour.'

Emily thanked the lady and then she was off.

The first room was a large hall. Emily raced round scanning all the labels on display, searching for any mention of a Harry or Dottie but disappointingly the labels only gave detailed information on the furniture. She made her way quickly into the dining room and began her search again with the same results, and again in the kitchen and the pantry.

She was about to head upstairs when she realised Cameron wasn't with her. She hadn't seen him since the entrance. Reluctantly she headed back the way she had come. She found him in the dining room studiously reading the label on the large dining table.

'I've read that one. It doesn't tell us anything about Harry and Dottie.'

He looked up and half-smiled at her.

'I was reading about the furniture,' he said. 'Believe it or not, I find it interesting.'

His half-smile turned into a grin.

'Oh,' she said, 'but I thought you didn't want to be here.'

'I can think of better things I could be doing on a Sunday morning.' He raised his eyebrows. 'But now I'm here I might as well indulge my weakness for beautiful furniture and enjoy myself.'

'OK, fine. I'll meet you in the tea room later.'

'Fine,' he said. 'See you then.' And he turned his attention back to the label.

★　★　★

An hour later, Emily was sitting by herself drinking a cup of tea and browsing a book she'd purchased in the gift shop.

'Find anything?'

Emily looked up to see Cameron approaching, carrying a mug of steaming coffee, a plate with two scones and a sheaf of laminated sheets.

Emily's stomach rumbled. She hadn't thought to buy herself anything to eat and she wondered whether Cameron planned to eat both scones himself. He put down his things and folded himself into the chair.

'I think so,' she said. 'In the sitting room there was a photograph of a young man in an army uniform. His name was Henry Logan. Henry could easily be 'Harry'. He was the last heir to Logan Hall and he died during the Second World War. There's a copy of the photograph in this book so I bought it to compare it with our photo and to find out a bit more about the history of the house.'

Cameron nodded.

'Yeah, I thought he had potential.'

'You did?'

'Yes, it's all here in the laminated sheets you ignored.' He tapped the pile. 'There's even a photo but apart from the fact both men are in uniform, it's impossible to tell whether they're the same person.'

She glared at him and took one of the sheets. Sure enough there was plenty of information about young Henry Logan who died at the age of twenty-four. She studied the picture intently. It had to be him, surely.

Cameron cut into the first scone and liberally coated the insides with butter and jam. He made a contented sound as he bit into it. Emily put the sheet back down.

'OK, so I've been reading this book and I've found another picture of Henry Logan with a group of young people,' she said. 'It's some sort of picnic. Anyway, he's standing next to this young woman. There's something in the way she's turning towards him that suggests they're more than just friends. She could be Dottie — see?'

She handed Cameron the book, which he put down on the table in front of him to study.

Emily eyed the remaining scone. Was he going to offer it to her? Should she just take it? When she looked back up she realised he was looking at her and not the picture. It was impossible to read the look under his gaze.

'Would you like the other scone?' he asked.

Embarrassed to have been caught gazing at the food, Emily said, 'No, no, thank you. I'm not hungry.' Her stomach rumbled in protest.

'How about we share it, then?'

'Oh . . . OK, thanks.'

Cameron started cutting the second scone.

'Well?' she said.

'Well what?'

'What do you think of the photo?'

Cameron sighed. 'I think, Emily, that this is all very tenuous.'

He pushed the plate towards her and she took a big bite. The scone was crunchy on the outside but soft in the middle, the butter was rich and the jam had the right amount of sweetness. She almost moaned in delight.

'I know you want this to be them, but all we've got is Henry Logan standing next to an unidentified woman. We don't even know if Henry was actually known as Harry.'

Emily finished off the first half of the scone and without thinking, picked up the second. She understood his scepticism but she refused to be despondent. She had a gut feeling she was right.

'We could ask Nana.'

'Who?'

'Nana, the lady at the desk.'

She popped the last of the scone in her mouth and looked up at him. His shoulders were shaking with mirth. 'What is it?'

'She's Anna.'

'Who is?'

'The lady at the desk is called Anna. Did you really think she was called Nana?'

Emily nodded and Cameron guffawed. Seeing his reaction Emily couldn't help but giggle, which made him laugh harder. She realised she'd not seen him laugh once since they'd met. Smile, yes — almost constantly — but not laugh. It suited him.

'Are we done here?' she asked,

gathering up the book and the sheets.

'So it would seem,' he said, standing up.

'Oh . . . em, sorry . . . I ate the entire scone,' she said, shamefaced. 'Can I get you another?'

'Don't be silly. I got it for you, anyway. I offered to share because some women . . . well some women can be funny about eating cake.'

'I'm not one of them.'

'I can see that.'

She hit him lightly on the arm with the laminated sheets but she was grinning.

Spending time with him was all right now that he wasn't trying to be charming. Maybe this summer wouldn't be too bad after all.

Anna couldn't help them with Henry's private life. All she knew was already written on the information sheet, but she did think there was a man who lived nearby who might possibly have more information.

'Paul Standen has lived in the town

38

up the road from here all his life,' she said. 'He used to tend the gardens at the Hall but he got too old for that. He's about ninety now, I think. I don't know his actual address but I can direct you to his house from here.'

Cameron was about to speak but Emily jumped in. 'Thanks, that would be great,' she said.

Ten minutes later they were on their way, clutching a map drawn in Anna's spidery writing.

As they made their way through an archway that connected the Hall's gardens with the town of Lentworth, Emily commented, 'You've gone very quiet.'

'This is an odd thing to be doing.'

'You don't have to come. I'm sure you could find some second-hand furniture shops to browse.'

'As if I'd let you walk down deserted lanes to some old man's house on your own. If something happened to you, your mum would kill me.'

Emily snorted.

'And I do have other interests than

second-hand furniture.'

'Oh? What are they?'

'I enjoy swimming, surfing, diving . . . pretty much anything to do with the sea, really. How about you?'

'Me? Oh, I like all of those things, of course.'

Emily didn't like to admit she hadn't really done anything since Johnny's death. He'd been the one who liked to try new things and she had thrown herself into every one of his schemes. They'd had fantastic fun and Emily, who'd had a fairly sheltered upbringing, found she had liked living a life full of adventure.

After the accident, though, she'd had to focus on just getting through each day.

She established a routine, which involved work — not as the computer programmer she'd trained to be, as that reminded her too much of Johnny — and watching television.

Had Johnny been around to see her, he would have been furious, she thought ruefully.

'You enjoy surfing?' Cameron's voice was full of scepticism.

'Sure,' she said. 'I've surfed all over the world. I think my favourite place is Bali because the sea is so warm.'

'And diving?'

'Oh, yes. It's so peaceful under the sea.'

Suddenly, she missed it desperately. She wanted to be on a boat with the waves slapping the side, Johnny laughing beside her as they pulled on their masks.

She stumbled and Cameron caught her, his warm fingers wrapping around her arm. She had felt no man's touch, apart from her father's awkward hugs, since Johnny and the feeling was unfamiliar — comforting and something else she didn't know how to name.

She righted herself and shrugged him off.

'You OK?' he asked.

'Fine.'

'Are you sure?'

'It's just ... I was remembering,

that's all. Sometimes it still takes me by surprise.' She didn't elaborate on what *it* was.

Cameron said nothing so she led the way down a narrow lane towards the High Street in silence, and then through the town and out into a country lane that twisted and turned as it made its way up a steep hill.

There was no footpath and as they walked in single file she was extremely conscious of him walking silently behind her. She racked her brains for something uncontroversial to talk about but nothing came to mind.

After five more minutes of walking, Cameron cleared his throat.

'Emily,' he said, 'I'd be very grateful if I could take you up on your offer to update the shop's website.'

She glanced back at him. His expression was pained. Asking for help hadn't come easily to him.

'Of course, no problem,' she said. 'I'll make a start later today.'

He cleared his throat again and said

gruffly, 'I'm afraid I won't be able to pay you.'

Emily waved her hand, 'I'm not expecting you to. Coming with me today was the payment we agreed. Besides,' she grinned, 'we're not going to find our couple here so there's more treasure hunting to be done.'

He groaned and shook his head but he was smiling, and the tension that had built up around them dissipated.

For the rest of the walk they talked about what alterations Emily could make and by the time they reached the cottage she realised his initial reluctance to update the website had been all about money and wasn't due to a lack of enthusiasm. Transforming the site would be fun, especially now he was on board, too.

★　★　★

The cottage they stopped outside was the only house for a couple of miles. The garden was a riot of colour with flowers bobbing gently in the breeze. One day, Emily wanted a garden like this for herself. She'd get cats to keep her company.

She pushed open the garden gate and the two of them went through. Before they reached the door a voice called out to them, 'Can I help you?'

Emerging from a vegetable patch in the corner of the garden an elderly man slowly made his way towards them. His face reminded Emily of a nut; dark brown and weathered by the sun and wind.

'Sorry it took so long to reach you,' the man said. 'My legs aren't what they used to be.' He smiled, his teeth bright white against his skin.

'I'm Emily, this is Cameron,' she said. 'We're looking for some information about Logan Hall. Anna thought you might be able to help us.'

'Anna, yes. I'll see what I can do. Would you like to sit?' He gestured to the wooden bench next to his front door.

They all sat, in a row, like candidates for a job interview. Emily repressed the sudden desire to giggle. Cameron was right; this was an odd thing to be doing.

'We found a piece of jewellery and a letter in an old writing desk,' she explained, 'and we're trying to locate the owners.'

The old man was suddenly no longer smiling.

'I'm not able to help you,' he said sharply, making as if to rise.

'Wait,' she said. 'The letter was from Henry Logan to someone called Dottie. Do you remember them?'

'No,' said the man, standing up. 'I never met Harry Logan or anyone called Dottie. Now if you'll excuse me I've lots of work to do.'

With that he walked off into his house, slamming the door behind him and leaving Emily feeling distinctly shell-shocked.

4

Cameron swept the rake over his father's grass. A few of the branches gathered into the pile he intended but most pinged off in different directions. He wiped his brow with the back of his hand. Even though it was evening he was still sweating profusely.

Why had he volunteered to cut Alastair's hedge on the hottest day of the year? And after a full day's work too!

His father's gardening skills were adequate at best and the hedge had been threatening to engulf his entire garden.

Alistair didn't want rent, which was a financial godsend, so Cameron had decided to help out in any way he could — but gardening was a crazy idea. Vacuuming the lounge now and then would have to do in future.

He took a slug of water; it was warm. As soon as these branches were under control he was going inside for an ice cold lager.

'Coo-ee, it's only me.'

Cameron looked up to see Maddie peering at him over their adjoining fence. Happily abandoning his rake he made his way over to her. She was always a joy to talk to.

'Now Cameron,' she said, before he'd even returned her greeting. 'Tom and I are having a little soirée next Friday evening at our house. You and Alistair must come.'

There was nothing 'small' about Maddie's soirées. They were legendary among her neighbours for good food, wine and gossip. Cameron had heard stories but he'd never been to one, so he wasn't about to miss this opportunity.

'We'd love to,' he replied, answering for his father as well.

'Great. I've invited a few people your age. I thought it would be good for Emily. She could do with a bit of fun after . . . well you know, you've seen what she's like. She used to be so bubbly. So, if you've any friends you'd like to bring . . . '

Cameron's mind wandered as Maddie chatted on. Before their trip to Logan Hall, he wouldn't have believed the barriers Emily had erected around herself could ever come down any time soon, but he'd seen a different side to her that day. Her whole body language had been different; she'd been excited, interested and engaged.

Maybe Maddie was right and all Emily needed was a little push to get her on the road to recovery. He hoped it was that simple.

'Hey there.'

Cameron looked up.

As if he'd conjured her, there was Emily next to her mother. He hid a smile, noticing that they were both so short that all he could see was their heads and shoulders over the low fence.

'Hi,' he said.

'I've just finished developing the website on my test server and wondered if you'd like to take a look at it before we go live.'

Before Cameron could respond, his father's patio door slid open to reveal Alistair wearing nothing but a pair of frayed denim shorts while clutching an array of brightly coloured shirts.

'Oh hello, Maddie, Emily. I didn't see you both there,' he said.

Instead of returning to the house and putting something over his bare barrelled chest — as Cameron would have preferred — he carried on walking, the grey hairs on his rounded tummy glinting in the sun.

'I'm glad you're here, Maddie. I've got a date tonight and I'd value a woman's opinion on which shirt looks best.'

He held up a short-sleeved orange shirt, the bottom half of which was covered in large pink flowers! What had possessed him to buy that?

Cameron glanced at Emily who was looking suspiciously tight-lipped. She caught his eye and quickly glanced away but not before a huge grin spread across her face.

Several more shirts were paraded,

49

each one more garish than the last.

At last Maddie finally said, 'I'm going to come round and take a look at your wardrobe, Alistair, and try to find you something more suitable.'

'Thanks, Maddie, you're a star.'

Maddie disappeared from behind the fence and Alistair went to let her in.

'Well,' said Cameron once he and Emily were alone. 'That's proof you can still be embarrassed by your dad even when you're in your thirties.'

Emily giggled. It was the second time he'd made her laugh in a week; he was on a roll.

'Your dad's great,' she said.

'He is, but I wish he hadn't come out semi-naked and shown your mum clothes he must have found in a bargain bin.'

Emily grinned and balanced her laptop precariously on the fence between them.

'Would you like to take a look now?' she asked.

'Sure.'

Looking at a computer balanced on a fence wasn't the best way to see the new site. He could invite her into the house but that might overstep those invisible boundaries of hers — and there was the risk of walking in on his father in various stages of undress.

Cameron shuddered; the fence it was, then.

He opened the laptop, Emily leaned over and ran her fingers over the mouse pad and the screen came to life.

'Wow,' he said. 'It looks amazing!'

The page was more feminine than anything he would have imagined himself, with a border of blue swirls, but it worked. The font was really clear and everything appeared to be organised logically.

He noticed links to social media sites and guessed she was setting those up too. He was incredibly grateful for all the work she'd done. Even if he doubled her salary, which he couldn't do, it wouldn't be enough to pay her back.

'If you click on these links here,' she said, pointing to the top of the screen, 'it will take you to the different ranges of stock.'

'May I?' He indicated that he wanted to take the laptop and sit down with it.

'Sure.' She nodded.

He took it over to his father's patio and sat with it on a wooden bench.

Emily leaned on the fence and watched him. 'Where did Alistair get that bench?' she asked after a few minutes. 'It's gorgeous.'

'Thanks,' said Cameron. 'Actually I made it myself a couple of years ago.'

'You did? That's incredible!'

He smiled at the incredulity in her voice; it wasn't flattering.

'Not as incredible as this site,' he said. 'You're a genius.'

'Thanks,' she said. 'I've been thinking though . . . you know that just relaunching the website isn't going to bring in many more sales.'

'True,' said Cameron, feeling slightly deflated.

'I was thinking you should have a launch party.'

'A party to launch a website? Do people do that?' It sounded expensive, which is not what he needed right now.

'Well,' said Emily, suddenly looking rather shifty, 'Please don't take offence at this . . . '

A comment which always preceded something offensive. He braced himself.

'The shop name doesn't really reflect the contents, so I think you should change it,' she finished in a rush.

Emily looked guilty, as if she'd insulted his firstborn — but in fact he agreed with her.

McKenzie & Brown's hadn't been his first choice. Paul had insisted that the name lent the business 'gravitas' and Cameron had been seduced by the idea of having his name on the shop front. Since Paul had left he'd been toying with the idea of changing the name, but he wasn't sure it was worth the financial cost.

He thought of the recent scarcity of customers and sighed. He should take this bold step. After all, it was sink or swim time.

He nodded. 'I agree.'

'You do?' Emily looked at him in real surprise.

'Something more practical would be good. I've been giving it some thought recently. I guess if we had a launch, we could get the local press involved, too.'

'Great idea,' said Emily. 'We could entice people in with a free glass of Prosecco. Oooh! We could run a competition with the winner announced on the day, or maybe a raffle . . . '

Emily was getting carried away.

The cost of this relaunch party was currently more money than he had in his bank account!

Maybe it was worth getting another loan. Or perhaps they could do the party as cheaply as possible while still making sure everyone had a good time. Was that possible?

He'd have to give it some more thought and crunch some numbers but the idea certainly had great potential to raise the profile of the shop — and he had enough sense to realise that was what he desperately needed.

'What names have you thought of?' Emily asked, breaking into his reverie.

'Home To Home — with the tag line 'Quality second hand furniture at reasonable prices'.'

'I like it.'

He smiled, shut the website down and stood up to give the laptop back to her. A travel page was now open on the screen.

'How's the trip planning going?' he asked as he handed it over.

'Good,' she said. 'Great, in fact. I've booked my flights. I'm going to New Zealand in September.'

He was surprised. As he'd come to know her, he hadn't thought she'd actually go through with the trip. She was a home bird, who was close to her parents.

He'd started to hope she'd stay with him at the shop and he was a bit disappointed that she wasn't — which was crazy because last week he hadn't even liked her very much!

'So you'll be leaving in seven weeks? How exciting!' He forced a smile.

'Yes,' she nodded, although not looking particularly excited. 'So, if you want me to help with the launch we'll need to get organised.'

'I'll sound out a few more people. My loyal customers will definitely have an opinion. Once I'm set on a name we could have some flyers done. I've a friend who works in printing so hopefully I can get a discount.'

'I can design something for the billboard. Any ideas on a date?'

'How about the end of August? That gives us four weeks to get organised.'

'Great,' she said. 'On a different subject, I was wondering if you're free on Sunday?'

He had arranged to go out for Sunday lunch with a girl he'd dated a few times, but . . .

'Yes, I'm free,' he said.

He'd have to cancel his date but he wouldn't feel bad about it. It was best not to think about how much he'd rather spend the day with his mercurial assistant.

'Great, I'd like to head to Lentworth again.'

He'd thought as much — she seemed determined to reunite Dottie with her necklace!

Presenting him with the work she'd done on the website before asking him was probably her way of buttering him up beforehand. She hadn't needed to — he'd have gone anyway.

'What are you going to do to get that strange man to talk? I doubt he has a website that needs to be developed.'

She smiled.

'I don't think we need to talk to him again. I want to take a look at the parish records to see if there's any mention of Dottie. Hopefully we can trace her that way. Anyway, I don't think Paul Standen was strange — he was just hiding something.'

'OK, Miss Marple, what's he hiding?'

'That I don't know. And even if we knew what it was it might be totally irrelevant to our search. But he definitely knows more than he implied.'

'Obviously, otherwise he wouldn't have gone from friendly to hostile faster than you can say antique necklace.'

'Yes — but it's more than that.'

'Oh?'

Emily's face was full of suppressed excitement.

'I only referred to Henry Logan — do you remember? It was Paul Standen who called him Harry. It looks as if we are on the trail of the right person at least.'

5

The church's spire loomed above the canopy of green treetops.

'It must be near here,' said Cameron as he pulled the car to a stop at the side of the road. 'Shall we walk the rest of the way?'

Emily didn't need to be asked twice. Quickly she unbuckled her seatbelt and stepped out of the car, away from the stifling heat. She pulled at her cotton dress and flapped the fabric trying to get some air moving against her skin. There was no breeze today and although it was still early the car had been tortuously hot — which hadn't helped the overwhelming sock smell!

'Shall we head down there?' Cameron indicated a path pointing in the general direction of the spire.

They crossed the road and headed down a steep path that was blessedly shaded on either side by tall trees.

'So remind me again why we're going to the church. Couldn't we have looked all this up on the internet?' asked Cameron.

'Some parish records aren't on the internet yet. This one isn't. The vicar's agreed to show us the records from the early 1920s. I'm guessing Dottie would have been born around 1924 and I'm hoping she was christened here. I thought it would be polite to go to the service first. Well, Mum thought it would be polite. It was her that arranged everything.'

'How did she manage that?'

'The vicar was once a locum at her church. He was very young at the time and Mum's maternal instincts kicked in. She all but adopted him. She rang him up to arrange all this — I listened in on their conversation and I think a few more seconds of being persuaded by her and he'd have willingly handed over his life savings along with the records.'

Cameron laughed, 'Your mum's great. I wish she was my mum.'

Emily knew Cameron's mum was still alive and that his parents were divorced but otherwise she knew nothing else. Surprisingly, neither did Maddie — even though they'd been neighbours for nearly a year.

'Do you see much of your mother?'

'Not really. I was ten when I moved to Brighton with Dad. It wasn't long after they divorced and she stayed in Edinburgh. It's not that we don't get on but it was such a messy break-up and she complains about Dad a lot whenever we speak. It's awkward . . .'

'Is your parents' messy break-up behind your avoidance of serious relationships?' The question was out of her mouth before she could stop herself.

'Ah,' he said. 'Not only a computer genius and Miss Marple, but also Freud.'

His tone was light and teasing but the look on his face said, *Don't go there*. She recognised it because it was the one she always wore when someone brought up the topic of Johnny. She changed the subject.

'I've been meaning to ask you why the pile of mirrors in the stock room aren't on display.'

'What mirrors?'

'The ones stacked on the shelf, to the left as you come into the storeroom.'

'Oh, those — they're just junk.'

Emily had picked them up a few times to take a look at them. Each mirror was bordered by beautifully polished wood and engraved with an intricate design.

'Are you sure? They look beautiful to me.'

'They're rejects. I made my gran a mirror for her birthday last year and those were the ones that didn't make the grade.'

'Why not?'

'I made a few mistakes with the design on the edging. I'm hanging on to them in case the wood comes in handy for something else.'

'But, Cameron, they're stunning. They should be on the shop floor.'

He shrugged. 'The mistakes leap out at me every time I look at them. They're not good enough to sell.'

'Well they don't leap out at me. I'm going to take another look at them tomorrow and if I still can't see any flaws they're going out for sale.'

'Em, whose store is it again?'

'It may be yours but in this instance I'm the one in charge.'

He laughed. 'OK, but I'll reserve the right to tell you 'I told you so,' when they're left languishing on the shelves.'

'They won't,' she said, confidently. 'So . . . how did Friday go?'

On Friday he had left her in the shop on her own for the whole day while he went to an auction. She'd had Saturday off so they'd not had time to catch up until now.

'I picked up some interesting pieces — and a few vases for your window display.'

'Great, we nearly sold out on Friday.'

'I noticed. Your arrangement worked well. The whole shop could do with a facelift actually. I'll have to work on that before the relaunch.'

Emily felt a surge of pride. She'd done it; she'd made a difference, albeit a small one. Now that she was starting to like Cameron she really wanted his business to succeed.

★ ★ ★

The church was packed. Reverend Long was popular. At one point during the service he pulled out a guitar and the congregation broke out into song! However, it was so hot and stuffy and Emily's eyes began to drift shut as the churchwarden conducted a reading.

She felt a sharp dig in her ribs and glanced up to see Cameron smirking down at her.

He leaned down and whispered in her ear, 'I think Maddie would be embarrassed if her daughter got chucked out of church for snoring.'

She snorted and his shoulders shook as the old man in the row in front of them turned round to see what the noise was about.

Her skin tingled where his breath had whispered along it. She reached up and scratched the sensation away.

The Reverend Long took his time saying goodbye to his parishioners. Emily could see why Maddie was so taken with him; he had a gentle, open manner.

She tried to be patient as they hung around inside the church waiting for him to finish but she realised she was failing badly when she caught Cameron smirking at her again. She stopped hopping from foot to foot and picked up a leaflet on an upcoming church fair.

'Sorry that took so long.'

Emily looked up to see Reverend Long finally heading towards them with his arm outstretched. They all shook hands.

'I believe you want to see some records,' said Reverend Long. 'Do take a seat and I'll bring them out to you.'

'This is taking ages,' Emily moaned as the vicar disappeared into the vestry.

Cameron laughed and put his hand on her arm. 'The letter you found is seventy years old. I don't think a delay of a few minutes is going to make much difference.'

He pulled his hand away as Reverend Long came back clutching a large hard-bound book.

Emily wished Cameron wasn't sitting so close. His touch was making her feel things she'd rather stayed buried. After today, she was going to do this hunt on her own. They were getting too close and spending too much time together. It would be awful if he got the wrong idea about their friendship. She needed to get their relationship back on to a work-only footing.

The vicar sat down and placed the large tome on the pew next to him. Emily's fingers itched with the desire to pick it up but the reverend didn't pass it to her. Instead he stretched out his legs and settled down as if preparing for a lengthy chat. Emily's shoulders sagged.

'Maddie tells me you're on a quest to reunite a lady with her necklace. How lovely! Do tell me all about your progress so far.'

Emily sank even further into her seat.

'That's right,' said Cameron, brazenly reaching over and picking up the records. 'I bought a beautiful antique writing desk some time ago . . . '

Cameron was off, painting a picture of their discoveries so far. In full salesman mode he made the quest sound so much more romantic than it had been but Emily didn't mind because as he spoke he casually handed her the book.

It was heavy. She placed it on the pew next to her and slightly turning away from the two men she opened the first page.

It smelt musty and the pages were browned with age. Her fingers trembled as she read the first page. She figured Dottie was probably christened Dorothy so she was looking out for both names. She was five records in when she came across the first child named Dorothy.

She slipped her phone out of her handbag, grateful that she'd switched it to silent during the service, and took a snap of the page.

Cameron and Reverend Long were still talking when she came to the end of the records. She tuned back into their conversation and realised they'd moved on to football and were debating the possibility of The Seagulls, Brighton's football team, moving up to the premiership next season.

She waited with her hand resting protectively on the records until the conversation ended.

Cameron glanced across at her and she nodded quickly.

'You've been such a great help,' said Cameron, standing and holding out his hand.

'You're done already?' The vicar looked surprised. He obviously hadn't realised Cameron had been chatting with him for over half-an-hour.

'Yes, thank you so much,' said Emily,

shaking his hand.

It took another ten minutes to leave the church and its verbose leader but eventually they stepped outside. The heat hit them. It was nearly midday and the temperature had risen another few degrees.

'You were brilliant,' said Emily once they were back on the path climbing away from the church. 'Distracting him like that. You were so casual when you took the records. Have you thought of taking a career change and becoming a criminal?'

Cameron gave a shout of laughter. 'You'd have to be my partner in crime. You were taking those photographs so smoothly he couldn't see. Why was that, by the way?'

'I didn't want to give him the chance to tell me I couldn't do it and I thought it would be quicker than making notes.'

Emily's stomach rumbled loudly. Cameron grinned.

'I'm starving too,' he said. 'Let's go somewhere for Sunday lunch. I think we passed a pub not long before I parked the car.'

She almost protested. Lunch sounded suspiciously like a date and even though he didn't do serious relationships, she wasn't interested in a non-serious one either. Then her stomach rumbled painfully again and she changed her mind. He knew how she felt about dating, after all, so she was being silly to worry.

*   *   *

Cameron was right — there was a pub not far from where he'd parked. It was an old building, deliciously cool inside, and the smell of food coming from the kitchen made Emily's mouth water in anticipation.

He found a table while Emily ordered them lunch. She insisted on paying as a thank you for driving. He didn't protest too much, which made her wonder just how hard he'd been hit financially since buying out his partner. Maybe the situation was even more serious than she'd imagined.

While they were waiting for their food to arrive Emily pulled out her phone and a notepad. 'I found ten Dorothys, no Dotties and three with Dorothy as a middle name, which I didn't rule out since my granny was Elizabeth but everyone called her Ann.' She pulled up the first record. 'I think this one is too old. She would have been thirty-two when Harry died.'

'Maybe Harry was into older women.'

'I'll keep her in reserve for now and concentrate on the younger ones to start.'

Two plates, piled high with thick-cut meat and roasted vegetables, were placed in front of them. Emily abandoned the records and took a huge bite of lamb; it was meltingly tender.

'Wow, this is amazing,' she said.

She ate half her lunch, wolfing it down as if she'd not eaten in months, before looking at the records again.

'Pudding?' asked Cameron when they'd finished their roasts.

'Definitely, I've had my eye on the crumble since we got here.'

'I'll get them,' he said before she could get up.

She carried on making notes and by the time he got back from the bar she was able to say, 'I've narrowed it down to five possibilities.'

'That was quick. What next?'

'I'll check the death records. I think that information is available online but it will be easier now that I have more information.'

She was being deliberately vague, determined to stick to her decision not to involve Cameron any further.

The waitress delivered their puddings. Emily's spoon cracked through the topping and slid into the soft fruit below.

'This,' said Cameron between appreciative mouthfuls, 'is one of the best dinners I've ever had.' Emily nodded in agreement. 'Speaking of good food, are you looking forward to your parents' party on Friday?'

Emily chewed slowly on her mouthful

of pudding pondering how to answer.

Normally she would say 'yes'. Her mum's parties were fun and had been since she was a small child. Everyone had wanted to come to her birthday parties because Maddie never did anything conventional. As an adult she'd loved going to the grown-up version and she still laughed at the memory of Johnny getting the straight-laced vicar from her mother's church to perform karaoke with him.

However, she knew that this one had been organised with the sole intention of finding her a man. Not that her mother would confess as such, but Emily had read through the guest list and saw that men outnumbered women two to one — young men. She knew, from previous match-making attempts, that some of those men were single so she guessed that all those on the list without a part-ner were too.

The dreaded parade of eligible bachelors had begun, which had led to Emily making the biggest decision of her adult life. She'd booked her flight to New Zealand.

Her mother had been shocked but not as shocked as Tom, who had disappeared into his garden for hours after she'd broken the news. She'd felt guilty but she knew it was the only way to stop her mother's well-intentioned meddling.

Besides, this trip was exactly what Johnny would have wanted her to do with his life insurance money. He wouldn't have wanted her to be wallowing in misery. She ignored the voice inside her which suggested he might have been cross with her for effectively running away.

'I take it from your silence the answer is 'no',' Cameron said.

'Mum's in matchmaking mode again.'

'Ah . . . '

'I suppose she means well,' Emily shrugged.

'But no one wants someone else interfering in their love life, especially their parents. Now if only we could get my dad to stop trying to get me involved in his dating escapades, that would be a result. Do you know what his latest scheme is?'

Emily shook her head.

'He wants me to go speed dating with him! Can you imagine anything more embarrassing? And he can't understand why I'm not keen.'

Emily laughed and Cameron went on to describe some more of his father's dating antics. Before long she was in stitches. She was so grateful to him for changing the subject and making her laugh before she dwelt too much on her dad's sadness and the enormity of her decision.

6

As yet another passer-by ignored the leaflet in his outstretched hand, Cameron muttered, 'This is going badly.'

'Don't be so pessimistic,' said Emily.

The plan was to shut the shop early and hand out flyers advertising the launch of Home To Home to the commuters coming off the trains at Brighton station.

It had sounded great in theory but the train station had been horrendous. Hot, tired commuters wanted nothing to do with flyers about second-hand furniture and walked by frowning or staring at their phones. It was amazing how so many of them were adept at avoiding eye contact.

So they had trooped down to the Laines hoping for a more relaxed crowd. The only difference so far was the lack of trains. The people were just as reluctant to take anything from them.

'No one is interested, Emily,' Cameron said, unable to keep the despair out of his voice.

'That's not true. Mum's handed out loads.'

He glanced across at Maddie, who was deep in conversation with a Rasta-farian. It was true that almost every leaflet Maddie handed out was accepted — it was just that every leaflet took about ten minutes as she stopped to find out the life history of the recipient!

Tom and Alistair — who had also come along to help out — were having as little luck as Cameron and Emily.

'This is a disaster,' Cameron muttered. 'It's a huge waste of time and money.'

Despite his words he smiled at a group of women heading towards him. Dressed in short skirts and high heels that caused them to wobble on the uneven cobblestones, they were wearing the uniform of girls off on a night out. He wished he could join them — not because they were pretty, which they were — but because he desperately needed a shot of something strong.

He was in luck, they were all in such a good mood they each took a leaflet and invited him to join them for a drink. He laughed and wished them a good evening as they merrily departed. He turned round to see Emily rolling her eyes.

'What was that look for?'

'There wasn't a look. Well done for getting rid of so many leaflets at once,' she said, before turning round and trying her luck with a young couple, who completely ignored her.

Despite her words her tone was less friendly than before. Cameron turned away from her and grinned. If he didn't know better he would think she sounded jealous. Maybe there was hope after all. Hope for what, he wasn't sure and he wasn't about to dwell on his own feelings. Since their first trip to Logan Hall their relationship had definitely improved. She'd laughed at some of his jokes and even made a few of her own.

She'd even put his mirrors on display and, to his surprise, some of them had sold and not been returned as faulty. She nagged him to sell more of his own creations, so he'd dug out some of the items he'd made over the years and discovered he had quite a range.

She made a display of some of the smaller bits, which would be suitable for gifts, but she wanted him to come up with some mirrors and photograph frames for the launch. She thought he should brand his work but he cringed just walking past the small display. None of it looked good enough to him. Even though he was deeply sceptical about selling his own work, he promised he would make more. He found time spent crafting wood deeply relaxing and he needed that right now. He was throwing everything at the launch and the thought of it failing was keeping him awake at night.

Emily was being amazing. The

amount of time she'd spent working on the shop's website went beyond the call of duty, especially as he wasn't paying her for it. She was forever updating the shop's Twitter feed with details of furniture despite the fact that their only followers were Maddie and a few of her friends. Cameron was forever in Emily's debt.

Spending time with her took his mind off the scarcity of customers but it was more than all of these things put together. Now that she was relaxing around him, he could see that underneath her prickly demeanour there was someone worth knowing. Was he willing to spend the time getting her to break down those barriers so he could get to know her even better? He wasn't sure.

One thing he did know was that he trusted her to look after the shop on her own. She was more than capable, which meant he'd been able to spend time sorting out stock.

He'd thinned out the furniture on the shop floor, moving some of it into the tiny storeroom at the back of the building and, on Emily's suggestion, created some room layouts to showcase the furniture in a home setting. She'd been right to insist it would look good — it did. And now there was more room to move around the shop. With the antique writing desk taking pride of place in the front window the shop was looking better than it had in years — better in fact than when Paul had been involved. A few months ago he'd have thought that impossible.

When he locked up at the end of each day, he felt a surge of pride as he looked at the shop. If only he could get people through the door, he was sure they would buy from him.

He tried to smile at the people passing by but his smile died quickly as yet more strangers looked straight through him, ignoring his outstretched hand. He needed to change his strategy if he was going to get through this large pile of flyers.

After what felt like an interminable

length of time he came back to stand next to Emily.

'How are you doing?' he asked.

'Not bad. I'm nearly halfway through mine. The dads have gone to the South Laines to see if they have more luck handing out leaflets to people heading to the restaurants. How about you?'

'I'm nearly out.'

He didn't tell Emily that after his success earlier he'd been targeting large groups of women. It seemed to be working for him. He was feeling slightly more optimistic than he had earlier but he wouldn't go so far as to say the exercise had been a roaring success.

'I'm dead on my feet,' said Maddie from behind them both. 'I think I'll have to call it a night. We're going to have a huge turnout though. Almost everyone I spoke to said they would come. Ah, here come the boys. I think we're all hungry. Let's get a takeaway and eat it at ours.'

Obediently everyone followed Maddie back to her house, stopping on the way to pick up a curry from her favourite restaurant. Maddie, never one to miss an opportunity, persuaded the owner to put a leaflet up in his window, as well as handing him a pile of leaflets to offer his customers!

Beside him Cameron could feel Emily cringe at Maddie's shamelessness. He grinned; it turned out it wasn't only him who got embarrassed by a parent's behaviour.

$\star$ $\star$ $\star$

The evening was still warm so they took the takeaway cartons into Maddie and Tom's back garden.

Tom's garden was as different from Alastair's as it was possible to be. In one corner, runner beans curled tightly around regimented sticks. In another, star lilies burst proudly from their stems. Everything was organised and yet it looked natural, as if seeds from diverse plants had fallen and sprouted by happy accident.

They were sitting on Maddie's wicker furniture with the soft, sweet scent of nicotiana wafting around them. The air was peaceful and even Maddie was quiet for once but Cameron was having difficulty swallowing. The pungent lentils from his Dhansak were sticking in his throat. He took a swig of lager but it did nothing to dislodge the sensation.

'Does anyone else want a glass of water?' he asked, standing and heading to the kitchen.

'Yes please, love,' said Maddie. 'The glasses are in the cupboard by the sink.'

As he waited for the tap to run cold he watched the others chatting quietly to one another in the garden. They'd all stepped in to help him this evening and spent hours traipsing the streets. He only had his thanks to give them in return and he felt it wasn't enough.

Like an idiot he'd put almost all his money into this relaunch. Not that he'd had a great deal of it to start with. The money he'd had from renting out his flat had gone on a new Home To Home sign that would replace the McKenzie & Brown's shop sign the day before the launch party. His tiny savings had gone on printing flyers that no one really wanted — and he'd yet to pay for the food and drink for the actual day.

He took a deep breath and leaned on the work surface. It did nothing to relieve the sudden tightness in his chest.

If this relaunch failed, he was sunk.

7

Emily was wedged into a corner of her parents' lounge. She hadn't sat down for hours as the settee and other seats were being hogged by her mother's party guests. She'd tried to escape to the garden a couple of hours ago but it was equally crowded out there so she'd retreated to the lounge hoping to find a seat.

She was tired. This week had been hard work, out every evening trying to hand out flyers for the relaunch. In her spare time she'd been working hard on the website and she'd created accounts for the shop on all the social media outlets she'd used in the past. She even had a few followers who weren't just Maddie and her friends.

Boxing herself in the lounge was a tactical error because Maddie had been able to bring eligible man after eligible man over to her with little chance of escape. Emily took a sip of wine and looked at her current companion who was tall and twig-thin with brown, wispy hair.

She couldn't remember what his name was and he'd just asked her a question that she hadn't heard because she was too busy thinking about Cameron and his shop.

'Pardon?' she said.

'I asked what you do for a living?' he said. Poor guy, this was as tortuous for him as it was for her.

He was the fifth man Emily had been introduced to since her mother's party had started. He seemed nice, he was a vet and had kind eyes, but she desperately wanted to get away from him.

'I'm a computer programmer,' she said. Why had she said that?

She hadn't thought of herself as a programmer for years. She'd met Johnny at university when they were both doing a computer programming degree, and now anything to do with computers reminded her of him, of late nights doing coursework, of days spent applying for their dream jobs and, once they'd got the careers they'd both wanted, helping to problem-solve one another's projects in the evenings.

It had been her life for many years but after he'd died she hadn't wanted to go back to her well-paid job and the career she'd worked so hard to achieve. Until recently she'd steered clear of programming completely. She'd worked in an art gallery as an assistant before she'd moved to Brighton.

So what had possessed her to call herself a computer programmer this evening? Why not mention her job at McKenzie & Brown's? She could have used the opportunity to get another person interested in the relaunch.

Or she could have talked to him about the travelling she had planned. She'd booked her flight from New Zealand to Cairns in Australia so she could dive at the Great Barrier Reef, something she'd always wanted to do.

Now that she'd booked the flight she was genuinely starting to look forward to going on her travels.

She could have mentioned any of these things — anything but the person she no longer was. Perhaps she'd said it because she'd been sitting at a computer for most of the day.

She'd taken the day off work to help Maddie prepare for the party but her mother had insisted that she didn't need any help.

Emily had taken it as a golden opportunity to do more Dottie research. Early on she crossed one Dorothy off her list because she'd died before 1940, the date on the letter. Another one had married before 1940. After much deliberation she'd crossed this one off the list too. Although she was keeping her on the reserve list just in case it turned out Harry had been in love with a married woman. It would explain why the letter had been hidden in a secret drawer. She really hoped not; it went against everything she'd dreamed up about the love affair between Harry and Dottie.

Now she was left with three women, two of whom were annoyingly both called Dorothy Smith and had been christened very close together. At first she'd thought it was an accidental repeat entry but the girls had different parents. It looked like both the Dorothy Smiths had become Land Girls at the outbreak of the war. She'd discovered that the National Archives in Kew would be able to give her information on where the Land Girls had been posted. She was hoping she'd be able to track the Dorothys from there.

She glanced across the room at Cameron who was deep in conversation with a raven-haired woman. The woman kept touching his arm and laughing at everything he said. He was such a flirt. Emily had decided she wasn't going to tell him she was going to the Archives. She was going into London by train so she didn't need a lift and anyway he'd told her it was her hunt right from the beginning. He wouldn't be bothered about coming with her.

The lounge was packed with people. It was difficult to hear what anyone was saying. She kept hoping to bump into someone she knew and put an end to the carousel of eligible bachelors. So far, no luck.

She glanced across the room again. The raven-haired girl had definitely taken a step closer to Cameron, so close Emily couldn't see the sideboard behind them. She'd have to ask Mum who the girl was. She didn't look like the type of girl he'd be interested in — too showy — but then what did she know? As far as she could tell, from what Mum had said and what she'd observed, he had a different girlfriend every couple of weeks.

She realised the tall man had drifted away, probably because she'd not been the most attentive listener. She was alone again — but her mother made sure that didn't last very long.

Man number six was called Alan, also tall with large doleful eyes. He brought all Emily's maternal instincts out, which was probably not the result her mother had been hoping for! By man number eight she was losing patience. Why couldn't Maddie just enjoy the party and leave Emily alone?

She looked around; everyone else was having a good time. Plates were laden down with food and no one had an empty glass. Tall Man was talking animatedly to an equally tall woman so the evening was probably a success for them both. There was no sign of Cameron and the woman he'd been talking to.

Emily glanced at the clock — it was nearing eleven. If Johnny were here he'd have been getting out the karaoke machine and she would have been looking through the song book to choose her party piece, which was a pointless exercise because her first song was always Madonna's *Material Girl*. Johnny would have chosen *Billie Jean* and he'd have sounded like a strangled cat — he'd been a terrible singer. She grinned.

'I'm glad to see you're having a good time,' said Maddie, appearing for once without a man on her arm. 'Have I introduced Alex yet? He's a doctor, paediatrics I think. Or is he a podiatrist? What's the difference?'

'One is feet and the other is a doctor who looks after children. That's quite a difference. And yes, you have introduced me. He's a podiatrist.'

'Is that the feet one?' Emily nodded. 'Oh, that's not a nice job is it? Can you imagine looking at feet all day? It's bad enough I have to see your father's but if I had to look at a stranger's — no, that wouldn't do for me at all.'

'It's a good job you were a nursery teacher then,' said Emily, smiling at her mother despite her exasperation.

'Ah, here's someone else I'd like you to meet. Nick,' she called out before Emily could stop her. 'Come and meet my daughter, Emily.'

Maddie performed the introductions before conveniently spotting someone else to whom she needed to talk.

Nick was not much taller than Emily with ash-blond hair, pale blue eyes and a permanent smile. He talked to her for a while about the party and then about his job as a store manager and, like the rest of them, he was a nice guy — just not for her.

Emily was worn down by a whole evening of trying to appear interested so as not to be rude, but not too interested in case they got the wrong idea. This was crazy! Why was she staying at the party? She should call it a night and go to bed. Mum might be cross with her but she wasn't able to stay mad for long. It would be worth a little row not to have to make small talk again.

While Nick talked about his geocaching hobby Emily's mind wandered.

She'd been toying with the idea of writing to her old boss, Don. He'd always said the company didn't want to lose her and if she was ever interested in coming back, he would find a role for her. Was it too much to email him and see if there were any opportunities for working for the company in their American headquarters? It would be a way back into her dream job, and living in the States would be sufficiently different so as not to be constantly reminded of Johnny. Was she brave enough to do it?

Right at this moment, she felt she could — but perhaps it was a reaction to this dreadful party. It would be less extreme to just go to bed!

Excusing herself from Nick, she made her way into her parents' hallway. It was blessedly quiet. She nipped into the loo to give her excuse for leaving some validity. After she'd finished she opened the door to find Nick waiting outside.

'Oh sorry,' she said, 'I didn't realise anyone was waiting.'

'I was waiting for you,' he said. 'Maddie told me you're single and I wanted to ask you out on a date before someone else snapped you up.'

'Oh . . . I, em . . . '

In all her twenty-nine years no one had asked her out so bluntly. Johnny had casually suggested they go out for drinks and before that any boyfriends seemed to happen spontaneously.

'You're the first girl I've asked out since my marriage ended. I decided to take the plunge because you're so beautiful.'

His eyes were full of trepidation and his megawatt smile was dimming as he waited for her response. She couldn't imagine what her facial expression looked like but she guessed it didn't look good. She didn't want to hurt his feelings but she desperately didn't want to go out on a date with this man. She was suddenly very angry with her mother for putting her in such an awkward position.

'There you are. I've been looking all over for you.' A warm arm slid around her shoulders and she looked up to see Cameron smiling down at her. He pulled her closer until they were touching down the full length of their bodies.

She frowned. What was he doing?

'I've come to tell you I'm off but I'll see you first thing tomorrow, babe.'

Then he leaned down and kissed her, very lightly, on the lips!

As he raised his head he winked at her and then he was gone, the front door slamming shut behind him.

'I'm sorry,' said Nick, 'I didn't realise you were seeing someone. I'm really sorry . . .'

The poor guy was red in the face and moving backwards towards the living room and the noise of the party. When he was by the door he turned and fled leaving Emily alone.

She touched her lips.

What on earth had just happened?

8

Cameron tried to stretch out his legs but his feet hit somebody's luggage. He pulled them back again and shifted in his seat. He glanced across the carriage to where Emily was seated, her shorter legs unencumbered by the cramped conditions. She was looking out of the window, watching the countryside whizz past totally unaware of his discomfort.

He yawned. He'd not slept well.

What had possessed him to interfere last night? It was a question that had haunted him through the night as he tossed and turned, unable to find a comfortable position.

He'd watched as Maddie had introduced Emily to man after earnest man, seen the way her shoulders had sagged and, as the evening progressed, how weary she looked. The party had been a real ordeal for her.

Maddie obviously meant well when it came to her daughter's happiness but in trying to force her to take an interest in a man she was simply making Emily miserable. She needed to accept that her daughter wasn't ready. Cameron had been looking for Maddie to have a discreet word with her about leaving Emily to make her own decisions when he'd found Emily cornered in the hallway by one of the eligible bachelors.

He'd overheard the man asking Emily out. He didn't think she would want to hurt the guy's feelings but he was confident she wouldn't want to go on a date with him either. So he did the only thing that came to mind. He pretended to be her boyfriend. He hadn't needed to kiss her, putting his arm around her would probably have been enough to scare the guy away, but once he'd held her close it hadn't felt like he'd had an option.

At least he'd only kissed her lightly. If he'd kissed her in the way he'd wanted to, he'd probably never have seen her again!

What had kept him awake most of the night was the realisation that he badly wanted to kiss her again. Thoughts on how to get around her self-imposed boundaries were tempered by the knowledge that she was leaving in five weeks for an indefinite period.

She'd been like a startled deer when she turned up at the shop that morning, all wide-eyed and stumbling. She hadn't made it far past the threshold when she'd stopped, seemingly incapable of coming in any further. She obviously wasn't desperate to be kissed again.

'Sorry I called you 'babe' last night,' he said, deciding to barge straight in with the elephant in the room. 'I thought it would send a message to that guy that you weren't interested, but who uses the word 'babe' any more? It's not the nineties!'

She'd given a little fake laugh.

'It did work,' she'd said. 'He backed off straight away and I was able to go to bed. Alone.'

'Good, great . . . '

They plunged into agonising silence. She'd clutched onto her handbag and stayed by the shop front door doing the little hop from foot to foot she seemed to do when she was anxious.

Should he mention the kiss? Would it make the situation better or worse?

The both started to speak at the same time.

'Sorry, you go on,' he'd said, grateful she'd spoken because he wasn't sure what had been about to come out of his mouth.

'I've found out that two of the three remaining Dorothys became Land Girls at the start of the war. The National Archives in Kew have details of where they went. They're open until five-thirty.'

'Great. We're always quiet on a Saturday afternoon. I'll shut the shop at lunchtime and we can head up there.'

Now, crammed onto a train with about a million tourists he realised she hadn't been asking him to come with her. She'd probably been about to ask him for the afternoon off!

He flopped his head back onto the head rest. He was making a real hash of this. He liked her — she was beautiful and intelligent — but she made it clear time and again that she wasn't interested in any kind of relationship. Once he'd closed the shop he should have gone for a run along the sea front and left her to it. Now they were in for a whole afternoon of embarrassment.

His phone pinged as a text message came in. He glanced at the screen and saw it was from Matilda. They'd been on a couple of dates last year and she'd been pleased to see him last night at Maddie's party. She was beautiful, fun and creative and she wanted to go on another date. He should text her back and arrange a night out. He would definitely do it later . . . definitely.

He put his phone back in his pocket and glanced across at Emily.

★　★　★

The train pulled into Richmond station and they joined the huge crowd leaving the platform. Cameron had lived in London for a few years straight after university but he'd never become used to the sheer volume of people. There seemed to be even more of them today, pushing towards the barriers, surging in from every side.

'Do you need me to help you at the Archives?' he asked as they queued with everyone else for the ticket barrier.

'I can manage on my own if you've something else you need to do.'

Yep, she'd definitely not meant for him to come. Heat crept up the back of his neck. 'I've a mate who lives round here. I'd like to call on him. I've not seen him in ages. So if you don't need me . . .'

'OK, I'll text you when I've finished.'

Her shoulders relaxed and he flinched in annoyance. Why hadn't she told him she didn't want him to come along? He could have done without paying for a train ticket. Now what was he supposed to do?

He trudged along the road towards Kew Gardens. He might as well do something interesting while he waited because he couldn't visit a friend who didn't exist!

As he approached he caught sight of the ticket price on a billboard — who'd have thought it was so expensive to look at some plants? He wasn't going to pay that price when he could go next door to Tom's house for free. So he bypassed the gardens and headed for the Thames.

He found a park bench and sat watching the huge body of water make its relentless push towards the sea. After a while he made some calls and used his phone to email a few people about house clearances.

He was about to head off to find somewhere to eat when Emily texted to say she was ready.

Still feeling irritated that he'd wasted his afternoon for no good reason, he took his time making his way back to her.

He eventually caught sight of her

standing outside the train station. She was clutching a large folder to her chest and she was doing the little hop thing again but this time she looked excited rather than anxious.

When he got to her he could see her eyes were shining and her cheeks were flushed. She looked as pleased with the world as when they'd found the hidden letter.

'Do you want a coffee?' she asked, when he finally joined her.

He glanced at the overhead gantries looking for the next train to take them out of here.

'Sure,' he said when he'd finally worked out which train they needed to catch, 'we've got more than half an hour before our train.'

They perched on high seats in the station's café and watched the trains coming into the station from the window.

He took a sip of the scalding coffee and it burned his tongue, 'How did it go?' he asked.

'I've found Dorothy.'

9

Cameron leaned through his car's window trying to show Emily the controls. 'It's a little bit temperamental,' he said. 'It doesn't like to be low on petrol and sometimes it stalls for no good reason.'

'I'll be fine, Cameron, I have driven before. Don't worry,' she said.

'Hmm . . . ' Cameron retracted his arm and stood on the pavement next to the open window. He was clearly regretting his decision to lend her his car for the day.

'I'll text you when I get there. And I'll text you again when I leave so you know when to expect me back. Promise.'

'Are you sure about this? This Dorothy might not be the right one.'

'I know. We've talked about this all week. It might not be her but I've a good feeling about it.'

'Ah. Well now I feel OK about the whole venture. You've got a good feeling, so it must be OK.'

She grinned. 'If you're that worried you can come with me.'

'Thanks, but I need to spruce up the shop before the launch on Friday. I might give it a lick of paint. If I don't finish today I'll probably close the shop tomorrow and carry on — so don't forget to bring your DIY clothes to work.'

She laughed. 'Thanks again for the use of your car. I really appreciate it.'

'Drive carefully,' he said and then turned to head back into his father's house.

She turned the engine — and the car promptly stalled. She glanced at Cameron's retreating back. His shoulders were shaking but he didn't turn round to look at her. She tried again and this time the engine spluttered into life.

She checked to make sure Cameron had gone inside the house and then wound down all the windows. She was grateful for the loan of the car but that didn't mean she could tolerate the smell for very long!

★ ★ ★

The streets around had once been wide enough for two cars to pass each other comfortably but now cars were parked tightly on either side. The second a space became available a new car swooped in to take it.

It took Emily ages to navigate the narrow warren of streets. She had to keep stopping and reversing to let more aggressive drivers through. It had been a long time since she'd been behind the wheel and every oncoming car made her feel jittery. She was glad when she'd finally navigated herself out of the city and onto open roads.

Soon she was whizzing along country roads, the breeze from the open windows sending her hair flying.

It had been easy to find out about the

Dorothy Smiths at the National Archives. One had been sent to a farm in Devon and the other to a farm near a village called Appleby, which was only a few miles from Logan Hall. She hadn't been able to find out a great deal about the Devon Dorothy but the other Dorothy had been extremely easy to track.

After the war she'd become a teacher in the local village primary school. She'd never married and as far as Emily could tell she'd remained in the village all her life. All Emily had done was Google Dorothy's name and Appleby together and she had come up straight away. The local church published a six-monthly newsletter that was published on its website. Dorothy was named as the editor and on the last page she gave her address for anyone who wanted to submit something for publication.

It had been so easy that Emily took it as a sign, although she hadn't mentioned that to Cameron. She didn't want him to make fun of her.

It was the fact that Dorothy had

never married that clinched it for Emily. She understood the absolute devastation of losing the love of your life. How your world never felt right again. How even looking at another man felt like an act of betrayal. Emily would never remarry and Dorothy had never found love again either.

It was just before lunchtime when she pulled into the village of Appleby. Emily reasoned Dorothy would still be at the local church service and so she pulled into a garage and bought herself a chicken salad sandwich and a bottle of water.

There was only so much she could take of Cameron's car so she parked it in a shady spot and got out her dad's East Sussex street map.

Appleby was tiny and the archetypal English village, with everything organised around a large green. Emily ate her sandwich while watching young cricketers play at the centre of the green.

Bright picnic blankets were dotted all over the grass as families gathered to watch. A mother chatted to her friend and her toddler took the opportunity to put his face in a yoghurt pot. Emily grinned as he emerged covered in pink goo. The mother carried on chatting, oblivious, while the toddler used her cardigan as a face wipe. Or maybe she had noticed and being covered in food was a normal part of being a parent. Emily wouldn't know.

She and Johnny had talked about having children but only as an abstract idea far in the future. They'd assumed they had all the time they needed to bring up a family together, but his death had robbed her not only of Johnny but also any children they might have had.

Shaking her head, she turned away from the happy families. She'd promised she would not play the 'what if' game any more. Johnny was dead. They wouldn't be having children and there was nothing she could do to change that.

She glanced again at the map. She

needed to head away from The Green towards a small group of houses set slightly away from the main village. But first she texted Cameron to let him know she'd arrived and that his car was undamaged. That complete, she headed off.

By the time she arrived at her destination she was a bundle of nerves. What if Dorothy wasn't pleased to see her? What if she reacted like Paul Standen had? Maybe the whole thing was better left alone — after all it had been seventy years since anyone had last seen the letter. Nobody would be expecting to see it again.

Then she remembered her words to Cameron, about how grateful she would be if someone turned up with something of Johnny's even if it was eighty years from now.

She squared her shoulders; she was going in. The hinges creaked as she pushed open the gate. She stepped through and the gate snapped shut behind her. A path cut through the neatly mown garden and led to a wooden front door. She rapped hard on the brass knocker and waited.

She was about to give the door another knock when it opened slowly. Standing in the doorway was a diminutive woman smartly dressed in a light grey pleated skirt and cream blouse. Her snow-white hair was arranged in a high bun and not a strand was out of place.

'How may I help you?' she asked.

'Hello, I'm Emily and I'm looking for a lady called Dorothy Smith who used to live in Lentworth until the early 1940s.'

The lady tilted her head to one side and looked at Emily for an uncomfortably long time.

'May I ask why?'

'Well, um . . . it's just, well . . . ' Emily took a deep breath and started again. 'The thing is, I found some property that I think may belong to her and I'd like to return it.'

'I see. Well you'd best come in then.'

Emily followed the lady into an immaculate lounge. China dogs adorned the mantelpiece and generous amounts of shelving space were dedicated to hardback books.

The lady gestured for Emily to sit on the floral sofa. She lowered herself down gently, afraid that if she moved too quickly she would upset the delicately balanced room. The sofa was surprisingly hard and didn't give way much when she sat. She put her handbag on the floor and rested her hands on her knees. The lady hadn't been all that welcoming and Emily was at a loss for words.

Cameron would have known what to say. He'd have turned on the charm and the lady would have been putty in his hands. She should have persuaded him to come with her. This wasn't so much fun alone.

'I'm Dorothy Smith and I did live in Lentworth from the time I was born until I was seventeen. I can't imagine what it is you think you've found that belongs to me.'

Emily cleared her throat, 'I found a letter in an old writing desk from someone called Harry. It was addressed to Dottie and I — '

'Ah,' Dorothy interrupted, her features softening into a smile. 'If you're speaking about the Dottie who was Harry's love you've come to the wrong Dottie. It's not the first time the two of us have been confused for one another, although I hadn't expected it to happen again in this lifetime.' She looked into middle distance for a moment, a smile playing around her lips. 'Oh, I'm sorry, you look terribly disappointed,' she said eventually. 'I'm sorry for my frosty welcome earlier. We've had trouble in the village with rather aggressive cold callers and I thought you were one of them. If you've time, perhaps you'd like to stay for a cup of tea and I can tell you what I know about the other Dorothy Smith.'

'I'd love to — thank you.'

Emily was glad for the sudden change in Dorothy's attitude. Perhaps today wasn't going to be a wasted effort after all.

Dorothy was gone for some time,

enough for Emily to wonder whether she should have offered to help. Eventually she heard the creak of a wheel turning and Dorothy returned pushing a trolley cart, the kind you used to see in restaurants when they brought round the pudding. On top was a china tea pot with matching china cups and saucers and, to Emily's delight, a large plate with a selection of mini cakes and pastries.

Once the tea was poured and they were both sitting there holding their teacups, Dorothy offered the plates of cakes to Emily.

'Please do take as many as you like. I made them for my coffee morning yesterday and I won't be able to finish them all by myself,' she said.

Emily leaned over and took a sponge cake. It was springy to the touch and had a light vanilla flavour. It was delicious. She took another one and tried to eat it slightly more slowly this time.

'Before I begin, perhaps you can tell me what it is you have of hers that you want to return?'

Emily told her all about the letter and the locket but she didn't get either of them out of her bag to show Dorothy. She wanted to hand them to Dottie and no one else.

'How romantic. I'll see what I can do to shed some light on the situation. Dottie and I,' she began, 'were both born in 1924 although I was a few months older. Dottie's parents moved to Lentworth about a week after she was born. I suppose they would have called her something else if they'd known there was going to be another girl with the same name living close by but it was too late by then. Our mothers became friends and so I don't remember a time before Dottie.

'We grew up to become best friends in the way young girls do. In school we were known as the two Dots because we were both so small. Dottie was beautiful — I don't mean to look at, although of course she was with her coppery hair and creamy skin, but she also had a beautiful soul . . . loving, kind and so passionate. She was full of life and always laughing. All the boys wanted to step out with her but there was only one who had managed to hold her interest.'

Emily held her breath.

'I can't remember his name now . . . gosh, and the two of us used to talk about him for hours!' Dorothy put her chin on her hand and stared off into the distance for a moment and then shook her head, 'No, it's totally gone from my mind.'

'Do you mean Harry?'

'No dear, Harry didn't go to the same school as us. He was too posh. I imagine he went to boarding school or was taught at home, I don't know. No, this boy was a smithy's son, I think. He was a year older than us and we were always making up excuses to go to the shops so that we could catch sight of him.

'I can still remember what he looked like; he was tall with dark skin and a wicked smile. Now I can't quite remember the exact sequence of events but I think she started stepping out with this boy around the same time she started work at Logan Hall. Perhaps a bit before. It was Easter time because I remember us getting told off for talking about it during the special service on Easter Sunday.

'She was thrilled, was Dottie. Not only did she have a job but she also had a man to take her to the dances. Any trouble in Europe didn't affect us in Lentworth. We had no idea war was brewing.

'We all knew about Harry Logan. Some of the girls in school would fantasise about meeting him and becoming his wife. It was all talk, of course. We all knew boys of his class didn't marry the likes of us. When Dottie started working at Logan Hall, everyone warned her not to let Harry Logan get close to her. We all knew that posh boys were only after one thing.'

Dorothy smiled rather wistfully before she went on, 'I don't know exactly what happened at Logan Hall. I got my own job around then so we didn't see as much of each other after that Easter. I do know that Harry *did* want one thing from her — but it wasn't what any of us were expecting. He wanted to marry her! And after a while she wanted to marry him too. As I said I only saw her occasionally after that Easter but she was so in love. I met him maybe twice, and he was just as besotted with her. They became engaged just before war broke out. Just imagine — if things had turned out differently Little Dot would have been Lady Logan.' Dorothy smiled sadly. 'Poor Harry. What a waste.'

'Do you have an address for Dottie?'

'I'm afraid I don't. We joined up as Land Girls on the same day and I was hoping they'd send us somewhere together but she ended up in Devon, whereas I was stationed down the road from here. Gosh, I've even forgotten the name of her farm now. Isn't that terrible?

'We kept in touch for a while. We

were still writing to one another when Harry died. She was grief-stricken, I know that. The last time I saw her was at his funeral. She'd all but disappeared, she'd lost that much weight.'

Dorothy was silent for a moment and they both sipped their tea, the clink of cups on saucers loud in the silence. Emily remembered what it was like to stand at your lover's funeral. Poor Dottie.

'We kept up correspondence for a bit but as the war dragged on, life got harder for all of us. We all lost someone we knew and loved. Eventually our letters dwindled to nothing. I expected her to come home after the war but her parents moved away and so I guess she had nothing to come back to.

'I can't understand what the letter and locket were doing hidden in a drawer. There was no secret to their affair. His parents were doting and there was no talk of them disapproving of the match, although I suppose they could have done. No, I don't think that was the case. His mother was clinging to Dottie at the funeral. Oh well, I suppose we'll never know . . . But if you do find out what happened to her and she's still alive, then please will you give me her address?'

'Of course I will,' said Emily warmly.

'I'll give you my 'phone number.' Dorothy slowly pulled herself to her feet. 'If you find out that she's died, please don't contact me. I know the chances are quite high — we're both in our nineties after all — but I don't like to think of someone so full of life not existing any more.'

Emily nodded and Dorothy left the room to fetch some paper. When she was gone, Emily helped herself to a little lemon tart.

'I found a photograph,' said Dorothy when she came back in. She sat on the settee next to Emily and showed her the black and white image. 'This was taken at a picnic in the grounds of Logan Hall. One of the two occasions I met Harry.'

It was similar to the picture Emily had seen in the book she'd bought at Logan Hall.

'That's me,' Dorothy said, pointing to a dark-haired girl sitting cross-legged on a picnic rug. 'And that's Harry and Dottie.'

Emily had been right; the girl in the picture who was standing closer to Harry than anyone else was Dottie. It was difficult to make out any features in the grainy image but the girl was petite with waist-length hair. She was smiling brightly.

She couldn't wait to tell Cameron she'd been right about the photograph. Of course she was going to have to tell him she'd been wrong about this Dorothy being the right one. Perhaps she could gloss over that bit!

'The others are our friends from the village. I don't know what happened to any of them, I'm afraid. You see this one, here at the back . . . ?'

Emily took a closer look at the image. There was a tall, dark-haired young man standing at the back of the picnic rug. Unlike the others he wasn't smiling.

'That was the man Dottie was stepping out with before she met Harry. He looks cross there but I don't remember any bad feeling between them. I think it's a bad photograph of him. It's much better with the digital cameras these days. You can take the picture as often as you want to make sure everyone's smiling.'

'Thank you for everything,' said Emily when she was eventually standing by the front door. Her handbag was full of carefully wrapped scones that Dorothy insisted she take with her.

'It was my pleasure. It was good to revisit the past. It's not often anyone is interested.'

Emily stepped onto the garden path, 'Well, I'll let you know if I find out any details of Dottie's whereabouts.'

'Thank you, dear.'

Dorothy stood inside the front door, watching Emily as she left. Emily had reached the gate when Dorothy called out.

'That boy,' she said. 'I've remembered his name. It was Paul Standen.'

10

Emily leaned down to dip her roller in paint. 'So he was definitely lying to us,' she told Cameron. 'But the real question is, why?'

Cameron looked down at Emily from his vantage point at the top of a stepladder. Her face was covered in tiny, cream dots. He'd finally found something she wasn't good at: painting.

He'd told her he was going to give the shop a lick of paint mainly as an excuse not to go with her to meet Dorothy on Sunday. He didn't want to tag along as he had the week before so he'd made sure there was no ambiguity; he was busy.

Once he'd started painting he'd realised what a difference it was making to the look of the store. So he'd made the huge decision of shutting the shop for the whole week before the relaunch and decorating throughout. He'd borrowed the money for the paint from Alistair and he was using Alistair's ladders and dust sheets — without him Cameron would be in desperate straits but he was looking forward to a time when he didn't have to depend on his dad.

So far Emily had been more of a hindrance than a help. He was redoing some of her edges, which, if he was being kind, could be called wonky. He'd given her a roller and told her to fill in the centre of the wall. She was better at this simple task but she was still incredibly messy. Her clothes were as paint-splattered as her face. It was a good job every part of the shop was covered in dust sheets otherwise the stock would be ruined. As it was, her hair might never be the same again.

'What?' she asked when she caught him looking at her. 'Have I got some of it on my face or something?'

'A little,' he said and then turned back to his corner before she could see the grin that split his face. 'So what's your next plan?'

'Well, she went to a place called Little Coombe Farm. I could go there and ask if there's any record of her. She may have stayed in the local village like the other Dottie. But it's in Devon, which is a bit of a trek.'

'Have you thought of just ringing them?'

'I've tried a few times but no one answers. I'll keep trying but I think my best bet is to try Paul Standen again. I know where he lives and he's not too far away.'

'He seemed pretty keen not to talk to you last time. What are you going to do to get him to tell you what you want to know?'

'I'm going to appeal to his good nature. He seemed sweet before we mentioned Dottie and Harry. Even if he was angry with Harry for stealing his girl, surely that anger would have faded by now — it's been decades — no one could hold a grudge for this long!'

'Maybe his caginess was because of something else entirely. Yesterday, Dorothy Smith thought I was a cold caller so it could be he was expecting something similar. Failing that I'll ask around. Now I've got a name, somebody has to know what happened to Dorothy Smith.'

'Do you want to borrow the car again? I only insured you for the day but I could extend that so you can borrow it when I don't need it. We can do that from now until you leave for New Zealand.'

She didn't answer immediately.

He glanced down at her again; she was concentrating very hard on a patch of wall, going over it again and again with the roller. 'Emily?'

'Um, well . . . ' she said. 'I was wondering whether you'd be free to come with me? To see Paul Standen, that is — not to New Zealand!'

He wasn't sure what to make of that. Had she not enjoyed driving or was it his company she'd missed? He wasn't going to play too easy to get. He looked down at her again but she was still concentrating on her bit of wall so he couldn't read her expression.

'I can't do this weekend,' he said. 'A group of us are going paddle boarding on Sunday. I can do the weekend after, if you like.'

'OK, thanks,' she said.

For a while they painted without talking, the only sound coming from the radio and the swishing of Emily's roller.

'Is paddle boarding one of the many things you're good at?' Cameron asked.

'I used to paddle board a bit.'

'Would you like to join us?'

'Thanks, but I sold my board a few years ago.'

'You had a board? So it *is* another thing you're good at. If you're interested in coming along you can hire one. That's what I do.'

'Have you ever done it before?'

'Never, but I surf. How hard can it be?'

She grinned, 'I think I will come along, then — I can watch you eat your words!'

He laughed and carried on with his edges. He still had tons to do if the shop was going to be ready on time.

It took them until Thursday afternoon to paint the shop. By then Emily's painting skills had improved a bit, or at least enough for her to paint sections of the wall without supervision, but to his amusement she still left covered in paint at the end of every day. The shop looked smart and fresh now, though — he hadn't realised how dingy it had become.

★   ★   ★

On Thursday evening Alistair came to help him move the furniture back into position.

'It's looking good, Cam,' he said as they put the desk back into its position in the shop window.

'Thanks, Dad. It's been a lot of hard work. I hope it's worth it.'

'Oh, aye, it'll be worth it.'

Cameron lifted a small table and set

it by the front door. Tomorrow every customer was going to be offered one free glass of Prosecco as they came into the shop. Maddie had kindly offered to hand them out and he had taken her up on the offer — partly because they may need the extra help but also because she'd coerce people into buying something. She was a born saleswoman.

He'd haltingly explained to her that he wouldn't be able to pay her. She'd patted him on the arm and said, 'You've already helped me more than I can ever repay. Let me help you now.'

He wasn't sure what she meant by that. If she was referring to Emily then he couldn't see that he'd been any help at all. Apart from giving her a lift a few times, paying her a pittance and giving her a kiss that had made her feel incredibly uncomfortable, he'd done nothing.

He'd said as much to Maddie — leaving out any mention of the kiss. She'd have marched them both up the aisle if she found out about that!

'You didn't see what she was like before she moved back to Brighton,' Maddie had responded. 'She was like a zombie, Cameron. Tom and I were desperate with worry but nothing we said or did seemed to make any difference to her behaviour. She seems to have made Johnny into this saint-like creature whom she's betraying if she enjoys life. The thing is, Cameron, he was a good guy, one of the best, and it's not fair that he died so young. He'd be the first one to tell Emily she was being over the top. He'd want her out there living life to the full. He'd want her to live, not just exist.'

'Well, she *is* going on this trip.'

'Yes, she's improved immeasurably since she started working with you. She's not as bubbly as she used to be but she's getting there.

'When she first mentioned she wanted to go travelling I thought it was just talk but now she's booked it and is making plans on what countries to visit. She's even talked about getting a work visa for the States. I'm pleased but Tom thinks it's too soon and that she's still fragile. He thinks we could lose her forever.' Maddie's eyes were bleak for a moment and then she shook her head. 'But Tom always tends to exaggerate the negative. I'm sure she'll be fine.'

For reasons he didn't want to analyse, Cameron wasn't keen on Emily going on this trip either, and now he was haunted by the words *lose her forever*. Was that possible? She didn't seem that fragile to him but if it were true that she had been almost zombie-like only weeks before they'd met, then she definitely wasn't ready to go.

The words *work visa* had also been like a punch in the gut. This wasn't going to be an extended holiday; she was planning to be away for a long, long time.

Cameron swallowed as he unpacked a cloth and put it on the table in front of him. It wasn't his business what decisions Emily made. She was a grown woman, she could decide for herself, and even if she did decide to stay in

Britain she was too talented to work as an underpaid shop assistant. He couldn't keep her here even if he wanted to.

'Would you like a drink, Dad?' he asked, keen to think about something else.

'I wouldn't say no.'

'There are two beers in the fridge. You get them and I'll put these plastic champagne glasses out. I think we're done for the day then.'

He heard Alistair go through to the kitchenette and open the fridge door.

'There's a mighty lot of Prosecco in here,' he called out.

'I'm being optimistic.'

Alistair laughed. 'In that case, have you asked her out yet?' he asked as he came back into the shop with two open cans.

'Asked who out?'

'Emily, of course. Or are you losing your touch?'

'She's a friend, Dad, that's all.'

Alistair snorted. 'There is no way you're not interested in such a beautiful girl. I've also noticed you've been suspiciously date-free since she's started working with you, even though you're normally a new-girl-every-few-weeks kind of guy. So what's the problem?'

'In case it's slipped your notice, I'm a bit busy at the moment making sure my business doesn't go down the pan. I don't have time for dating. As for Emily . . . well, aside from the fact that she's still grieving for her dead husband, she's not the type of girl you mess around with. She'd want something serious.'

'What's wrong with serious? You're in your thirties, Cam — it's about time you settled down and had children.'

Cameron looked at his father, who was swigging his beer straight from the can.

'Are you kidding me?' he asked incredulously.

'What's that supposed to mean?'

'My early childhood was spent living in a war zone! Why would I inflict that on anyone, let alone a small defenceless baby?'

'Ah,' said Alistair, leaning on the shop's counter. 'Well I suppose your mother and I aren't the best role models for marriage — but we had you and that made the whole experience worthwhile. But look at Tom and Maddie. They've been together since they were in their teens and they're still in love.

'My marriage wasn't great but that doesn't mean I'm against the whole idea, you know. If I find the right someone, I wouldn't hesitate to tie the knot again.'

'Really?' Cameron hadn't realised his father's serial dating was anything more than a bit of fun.

'Really. Doesn't mean I can't have a bit of fun while I try to find her though, does it?' Alistair grinned and Cameron laughed.

★   ★   ★

Cameron knocked lightly on Maddie's front door at six o'clock on the morning of the launch.

Emily opened the door almost

immediately. She must have been ready and waiting. She looked perky and fresh, whereas he'd had to drag himself out of bed when the alarm went off and he was still finding it difficult to keep his eyes open over half an hour later.

'Morning,' she said brightly and she stepped outside to join him. The morning light shone directly onto her hair making it appear like a halo of gold around her head. She took his breath away.

'You're chirpy for such an early start,' he said.

'I like early mornings. The world is at its best when most people are still in bed and you can hear the morning chorus.'

'You're weird.'

She laughed and they headed down to the promenade together.

'Nervous?' she asked as they headed along the waterfront towards the city centre.

'A little,' he said. Well, actually, a lot — but he wasn't going to admit he'd barely slept for worrying whether anyone would turn up. This not sleeping was turning into a habit. He'd slept like a stone before meeting Emily.

'OK, let's run through the day,' she said. 'We'll go and finish setting up now, Mum will arrive at nine-thirty, and we'll open at ten.'

'Alistair's on standby in case we do get a deluge of customers.'

'I'm sure we'll need him. We've got Annabel from the Argus coming to take photos and to do an interview at eleven. Then hopefully we'll be busy with lots of new customers all day. Then at six-thirty we'll bring out nibbles and announce the winner of our raffle. We can close at seven-thirty. It'll be fun, don't worry.'

'And if no one turns up we can get drunk on a shed load of Prosecco.'

She laughed. 'They'll turn up. We might have to work hard to get them interested in furniture, but I mean, who's going to turn down a free glass of Prosecco?'

He laughed. She was in a good mood

and it was infectious and suddenly he wasn't worried any more. He'd done all he could to make today a success, so if it wasn't . . . well, he'd worry about that tomorrow.

Emily hung up bunting and put the raffle prizes out once they arrived at the shop. Cameron, his resolve not to worry failing almost immediately, paced back and forth, knocking into the table displaying his own work.

'We should take this down,' he growled. 'It's all rubbish.'

'Don't be silly,' said Emily, coming to stand next to him. 'Everything on this table is beautiful and it's not going anywhere unless a paying customer carries it out of here.'

He began pacing again and glanced at the clock. It was only just after nine. This morning was going so slowly!

'The time's not going to go any faster just because you keep looking at the clock,' Emily said, glancing over at him.

'I think the clock has stopped.'

'Why don't you ring Alistair and see

whether he can come down?'

'There's optimism and then there's stupidity.'

She laughed. 'Stop being such a grouch. Ring him. In a worst case scenario he can help us drink the Prosecco.'

Alistair arrived with Maddie just before ten and after that time sped up remarkably.

Before he knew it Cameron was unlocking the shop door and was stunned to find there was a queue of people waiting. It was a small queue, but a queue nonetheless. Instead of inviting them into the shop he stood there looking at them all.

'Come in, come in,' said Maddie, walking around him and taking control. 'Come and enjoy a glass of Prosecco and browse the store.'

The customers fanned round him and followed Maddie into the shop. After a moment he followed them. Inside, Emily was grinning at him from behind the counter.

Alistair immediately homed in on an

attractive older lady to whom he was talking animatedly and waving his hands around as he showed her round a bedroom suite. He looked like a lunatic but the lady was hanging on his every word.

Even if this small crowd bought a few items and no one else turned up, Cameron thought he could count the day a success. This was more custom than he'd seen in ages.

An few hours later Emily came up to him as he was arranging the delivery of a wardrobe to an elderly couple.

'We're running out of Prosecco,' she said after he'd said goodbye to the pair.

'What? But I bought tons of the stuff!'

'It's been very busy. I rang Dad and he can pick up some more for you. I said I'd ring him back to confirm you're happy with that.'

Cameron looked around the shop. It was packed with people. Two women were having a polite but quite serious fight over a sideboard. He stood up to intervene. He had a similar one in the storeroom, so hopefully he could sell two.

'Tell him we definitely need more.'

She grinned and left him to it.

★   ★   ★

Cameron finally locked the shop doors at eight o'clock that evening.

'It was a huge success!' Emily cried. She was beaming and he realised he was severely tempted to cross the room and pull her into his arms.

Instead he said, 'We did it. I wouldn't have even attempted anything like that if you hadn't pushed me into it. So, thank you. Shall we all go for chips to celebrate?'

'That sounds like a great idea to me. Mum, Dad . . . ' she called out, 'Do you want to come with us for fish and chips?'

'I'm dead on my feet, love. Dad and I are just going to get a taxi home.'

'How about you, Alistair?' asked Emily.

'I've got a date tonight,' he said, giving Cameron a wink behind Emily's back. Cameron rolled his eyes as he caught Maddie smirking at Tom. He knew that if Emily even suspected this might be a date, she'd be moving her flight to New Zealand forward!

'Let's grab some on the way home,' he said, trying to keep the evening as un-date-like as possible but unwilling to let her go home in the taxi with her parents.

'Sounds great,' said Emily, unaware of all the smirking going on in the room. 'I'll get my bag and then I'm ready. I'm starving.'

Emily headed into the storeroom and Maddie clapped her hands excitedly.

'It's not a date, Maddie,' Cameron hissed.

'I know but she's so relaxed with you. It's fabulous. Let's go, Tom, before she changes her mind.' Maddie stood on her tiptoes to kiss Cameron on the cheek and then she shot out of the door, dragging Tom and Alistair with her.

'Where did everyone go?' asked Emily when she came back in moments later.

Cameron cleared his throat. 'The taxi came,' he said, hoping they weren't all going to be loitering outside when he and Emily left.

'Look at all these sold stickers,' said Emily as she weaved her way through the shop, stopping by the table of his own work. 'See, I was right about your work. All of the mirrors sold today and I even took a couple of commission orders. You should make a lot more of this.'

'I'll concede that you were right, once again,' Cameron said. 'I'll make up some more mirrors and some photograph frames and we can keep them in stock for a trial run. In fact the whole day was fantastic. Nearly everything on the shop floor has sold. I'll need to bring in more stock from the store room tomorrow.'

'I was trying to update the website as we went along but it still got away from me. I'll need a better system for tracking stock, I think.'

'We'll worry about that on Monday,' he said, locking the door and pulling the shutter down. 'For now let's concentrate on getting those chips.'

★ ★ ★

The promenade was thick with tourists shuffling slowly along in the late evening sunshine. Cameron wasn't in any hurry for the evening to end.

'Shall we get chips on the pier?' he suggested. 'We can find a bench and watch the crazy people on the rides.'

'Have you even been on any of the rides?' she teased as they joined the swell of tourists heading for the pier.

'When I was a kid I went on a few of them but I haven't in years.'

'Have you ever been on the Booster?'

'Is that the giant stick that takes you miles up into the air before turning you upside down, dangling you over the sea and spinning you round and round?'

146

'That's the one.'

'Oddly enough, no. What sane person would do that for enjoyment?'

She grinned up at him. 'Wimp,' she said.

'I don't believe you've been on it!'

She laughed, 'Of course I have. I'm not scared of a tiny ride like that.'

'That's fighting talk. Let's see you on it.'

'I'll do it if you do.'

Now he'd done it! He couldn't not go on the ride now or else he'd look like the wimp she'd accused him of being. The thing was it was incredibly high and he wasn't all that keen on heights.

'OK . . . ' he said, hoping the ride had closed for the evening and he'd be let off the hook.

'Great! It's fun — you'll love it.'

He doubted that very much.

Unfortunately for him the ride was still open and, because not many people were crazy enough to go on it, there was no queue.

He stood at the bottom and looked

up. The ride stretched up for miles. He turned to tell her that this was a bad idea but she was already bounding forward with the enthusiasm of a spring lamb. He cursed under his breath and followed her hoping that he didn't disgrace himself by screaming like a small child.

'Are you sure about this?' he asked, as the safety harness was pulled over their shoulders and clipped into position. 'It's not too late to change your mind.'

'Are you scared?' She turned to look at him. She was grinning and for the second time that day she took his breath away.

'Me?' he said. 'No way.'

She laughed and the ride slowly began to pull them both backwards. He made a noise somewhere between a 'wah' and an 'ooh' and Emily began to giggle uncontrollably. They made it to the top and he had a moment to admire the stunning views of Brighton and the bright blue of the English Channel before the ride sped up and plunged them face forwards towards the ground!

The next minute-and-a-half was a blur of sky, sea and floor as he was spun round and round, facing each of them in turn.

Then the ride stopped with them suspended miles away from the ground.

'What's happening?' he cried anxiously. 'Are we stuck?'

'No,' said Emily, between giggles. 'They're letting the people at the bottom off first.'

Sure enough tiny ant-like people were walking away from the ride as if nothing had happened to them. He wasn't sure his legs would ever work again, even if they did ever manage to make it down from this height.

'This is part of the ride. Enjoy the view,' Emily encouraged.

They were sitting facing the English Channel. The sun was setting across the water, sparkling in the fading light. It *was* stunning — but the view would have been as good from the pier. He could be eating chips now and gazing out to sea from the safety of the ground.

After an eternity the ride slowly began its descent and finally they were allowed to get off.

Cameron leaned casually against a rail while he waited for Emily to put her bag over her shoulder. It was just as well her strap caught in her hair and she had to disentangle herself because he wasn't sure his legs would have taken him far.

By the time she was free from her bag he was sufficiently recovered to walk to a chip stand and order them both takeaway fish and chips. They found a bench and sat down facing the sea.

'You hated that,' she stated as they opened their packets, releasing the smell of vinegar.

'No, it was fine. I particularly enjoyed hurtling face forwards to the ground. I think my life only flashed before my eyes ten times.'

She snorted. 'Thanks for the chips.'

'I'm just glad I'm still alive to be able to buy them for you.'

He tensed as he realised what he'd said but she just laughed and they ate the rest of their dinner, shoulder to shoulder, in contented silence.

'Do you fancy a drink on the beach before we head back?' he asked. 'My treat to say thanks for all the work you did today,' he added quickly before she thought this was straying too close into date territory. He thought it might be, but he didn't want to scare her away.

'I'll get a Whippy too,' she said. 'Would you like one?'

'A Whippy and a lager? That doesn't sound like a great combination.'

'Don't knock it 'til you've tried it.'

'OK, I'll meet you on the beach in a minute. If we sit on the beach down from the Salt Bar I can get the drinks from there.'

The queue for drinks stretched outside the bar and onto the pavement, so he stood in line and waited. What did he think he was doing? He was creating some sort of date with a woman who didn't date and who was going to the other side of the world in three weeks' time.

When had this started to be more than a passing attraction for him — and what was he going to do about it? The sensible thing to do would be to get a small drink, finish it quickly and get a taxi home.

'I bought a bottle of Prosecco,' he said, as he joined her on the pebbly beach. 'Hope it's OK.'

He half expected her to say 'no' but she took the bottle from him as he sat. Her other hand was slowly being covered in soft vanilla ice cream. 'Hopefully it will help take away the pain from these pebbles,' she said, as she handed him his ice cream.

He couldn't take his eyes away from her hand as she licked the ice cream away. This was getting ridiculous — he was acting like a schoolboy with his first crush!

'Yeah, sitting on the beach always

sounds like a better idea than the reality,' he said. 'Especially when it's a pebble beach.'

He licked his ice cream until the melting was under control, then he took the two plastic glasses out of his pocket and poured them each a drink.

She took a sip. 'Mmm,' she said. 'This reminds me of ice-cream soda. Not a bad combination actually. Better than lager would have been.'

He finished his ice cream in several bites and then reached for the Prosecco. They were halfway through the bottle and both lying with their backs to the beach looking out to the sea when she brought up the subject of Johnny . . .

'It was Johnny who took me on the Booster ride the first time,' she confessed. 'I admit I was terrified at first but then I got such a buzz from the thrill of it that I became a bit of a roller coaster addict afterwards. I never tried any of the rides on the pier growing up. I was too scared. I think Mum was so nervous about anything happening to her only child that she passed her anxiety on to me. Maybe if she'd had six children as she planned she'd have been a bit more casual.'

Cameron knew Maddie and Tom had only been able to have Emily but he didn't know why. Not wanting to open that can of worms, he asked her about Johnny instead.

'So how did he manage to persuade you to go on it?'

'Much like what I did to you today. He didn't give me a chance to say 'no'.' She smiled as she remembered. 'He was like that, wanting to try new things and not really caring about his own safety. That's what got him killed in the end . . . '

Cameron sat very still. He wasn't sure what to say. He'd never dealt with grief and this was so upfront and personal that anything he said now would be inadequate.

'He went out climbing with a friend,' she continued. 'He was a good climber, he'd been doing it since he was young, so I didn't even think twice about it. I was working on some stupid project for work. What haunts me the most is I didn't even look up from the computer when he came to kiss me goodbye. I told him to have fun and then I carried on with what I was doing.

'It was an accident . . . a tiny accident . . . he slipped and hit his head. He should have been wearing his helmet but he'd taken it off to scratch an itch. He wasn't even climbing at the time. They'd reached the summit and he was standing there when he lost his balance.'

She took another sip of her drink. It seemed to Cameron as if she'd forgotten he was there.

'He never regained consciousness. I sat by the hospital bed for days talking to him, asking him to stay with me but in the end they told me he was brain-dead. I had to make the decision to switch the life-support off.'

She was silent for a while and then she said with a hint of a smile in her voice, 'Compared to that, a ride on the Booster is a walk in the park.'

Her glass was empty. Cameron picked up the Prosecco and poured her a full glass. He needed to pick his next words carefully.

'Nothing I've experienced has ever been as terrible as that,' he said, 'which probably explains why I screamed like a girl the whole time we were on that ride.'

She burst out laughing. 'Don't tell Maddie she was right or she'll never stop going on about it, but coming to Brighton has been good for me. I'm starting to feel so much more like myself again and that's at least in part because of you. Thanks for being such a great friend.'

The trouble was, he was starting to want to be so much more than just her friend.

11

Perched on her makeshift desk of a few cardboard boxes in Home To Home's storeroom, Emily pulled Dottie's locket out of her handbag and held it up to the light.

The patterns on the surface were familiar to her now, as was the picture of Harry inside, but she still found herself looking at the piece at least once every day. She flipped the locket open. The image was small and faded but she could just make out the serious face of a young man in his army uniform. How would Dorothy react after seeing her necklace and the photograph for the first time in seventy years? She closed the locket and put it back in its protective case before dropping it into her handbag.

She turned to her laptop and switched it on. She'd told Cameron she was going out to the storeroom to update the website so she'd better get on with it. Not that he'd be cross with her if he found her not doing it. He was a very relaxed boss but she was leaving soon and she wanted to help him out as much as she could.

In the four days since the relaunch the shop had seen a steady run of customers with sales on the website slowly increasing as well. She had to change the site so that as soon as an item sold in the shop, it disappeared off the site automatically. She should have done that to start with, but she hadn't expected the relaunch to be such a success.

She was thrilled that it was, of course, but now they were so busy she hardly saw Cameron and even when she did all they talked about was ideas to promote the store and stock issues. Working in the shop was nowhere near as much fun as it had been the week before the launch, when they'd been closed and had no customers at all.

She was looking forward to Sunday and their trip to Lentworth. Not just because it might provide some answers as to what had happened to Dottie, but also because she could spend some uninterrupted time with Cameron. That was a secret she was taking to the grave because if it got back to Maddie, she would be booking the church and ordering a mother of the bride outfit!

It wasn't like that, Emily told herself firmly. She enjoyed his company, that was all. He was the first proper friend she'd made since Johnny's death and one of the few people who didn't treat her with kid gloves.

'Hey,' Cameron said from the doorway of the storeroom. 'How's it going?'

'Good — we've had another couple of online orders. They're small so I can pack them up and send them out by myself. We've also had two queries about stock but they're pretty simple so I can answer them myself, too.'

'Great. I'm pleased with the way the website's generating orders. I've not had much success with that before now. And before you say anything I know the site was out of the ark before, you've told me more than once.

'I've had a phone call from a guy who wants me to take a look at his late mother's possessions. From his description on the phone it sounds like he has some great pieces, but it's quite far away so I'll tie it into a visit to an auction house in the same area to save making two trips.

'However, it does mean I'll be away from the shop all day. I'm going to head down there tomorrow because I don't want anyone else to snap up the pieces. I've rung Dad and he can come in tomorrow afternoon if you think you'll need the help.'

Emily's heart sank at the thought of being in the shop on her own for the whole day. It would be boring without him.

'If you don't mind me leaving any online orders until the day after, I should be OK on my own. I don't want to put Alistair out,' she said.

'Dad has discovered that being in the shop opens a whole new avenue of dating channels he'd not thought of before. He's chomping at the bit to come down here again!'

Emily laughed. 'OK, then, invite him down. I'll try not to cramp his style.'

'When you've got a minute will you take a look at the wording for this flyer?'

Cameron had decided to run a course from the shop on how to upcycle old furniture. Emily loved the idea and would have signed up if she'd been around in September. She wanted him to run one on basic carpentry skills but he didn't believe he was good enough. She couldn't understand why. His designs were beautiful, he was so talented yet he couldn't see it.

'Sure,' she said. 'I'll take a look for you now.'

She jumped down from the boxes and made her way over to Cameron. He had a large bruise on his left cheek where he'd been hit by a paddle board at the weekend.

'How's the face?' she asked.

'Fine,' he said, 'barely noticeable.'

She'd noticed he didn't like to admit to any weakness. The fact that he'd accepted her help with the relaunch of the shop showed her how bad things must have been. She hoped the resurgence in customers continued long after the launch had faded from everyone's memory. He deserved it.

'And your pride, has that taken a bashing?' she teased.

'Not at all. I'm absolutely fine with being the worst of everyone I know at paddle boarding. I was glad to have provided everyone with light relief as I fell off the board again and again.'

'And again!' said Emily laughing.

At first she had regretted agreeing to go paddle boarding with Cameron and his friends. She'd worried an all-male group would regard her as his girlfriend. It had taken her long enough to get over the embarrassment of that fake kiss, so she didn't know how she would react to people thinking they were an item. She'd considered cancelling but the allure of being out at sea with nothing but a board and a paddle had overcome her reluctance.

Then she'd met Cameron's friends and found she'd not needed to worry at all. Sunday had been another hot day in this glorious summer and as soon as she'd woken up she'd been desperate to get into the sea to cool down.

She'd walked with Cameron from their parents' houses to the pier where they were to meet up with everyone else. On the walk there, their conversation had been easy and she found it hard now to remember her indifference to him in the beginning. She'd thought him shallow but the more time she spent with him proved her wrong.

His friends, who'd all called him Cam, were a mixed bunch from very diverse backgrounds. The only thing they all seemed to have in common was a really relaxed attitude to life. No one commented on her relationship with Cameron.

He had been talking to his friend, Louisa, about their mutual love of surfing from the moment they'd all met up until they'd all got their paddle boards and were about to head into the water. From what he was saying he was a competent surfer so Emily was expecting him to be a natural on the paddle board.

He was not.

Ten minutes into the experience and she was laughing so hard she had to get off her own board because she could no longer stand upright!

Tears of laughter were running down her face as he slid onto the board and straight back off again, head first into the water. But he'd not given up, not even when his board flipped sideways and hit him in the face so hard he was knocked backwards. He'd kept getting on until he'd mastered it — and when he had, he was better than everyone.

They had made their way further

away from the shore than the others. Cameron was in front and Emily thought how well the wetsuit suited him — all black and clinging to his muscular frame. His dark hair was drying in small tufts all over his head but even that didn't detract from his attractiveness. She could understand now why female customers went a bit funny when he turned his charm on them.

Now, in the shop, she was standing so close to him she could see the faint smattering of stubble pushing through the bruise where it was obviously too painful to shave.

She looked up at him to tease him some more but when she caught his eye she found it difficult to breathe. He was looking down at her intensely. Suddenly his gaze flickered from her eyes to her mouth and back again — but so quickly she could have imagined it. Was he thinking of kissing her?

She froze. She couldn't decide if she wanted him to or not. No, she didn't want him to. He wasn't Johnny and she'd made a promise, but even with that thought foremost in her mind she still couldn't move.

The bell to the shop door tinkled and the spell was broken.

Cameron handed her the flyer and went into the shop floor to see who'd arrived.

Emily scurried back to her computer. Her fingers shook slightly as she responded to an email about a modern writing bureau. She tried to concentrate but her mind kept slipping back to Cameron.

This reaction to standing close to him was crazy. Nothing had actually happened. Neither of them had moved and it had all happened in seconds — if, indeed, anything had happened at all. By the time she was ready to go back into the shop she'd convinced herself that the whole episode had been just her imagination.

Cameron was talking to a young couple about the antique writing desk. That wasn't unusual, most customers who came in took a look at it — then they saw the price tag and walked on. Those customers who had time to spare wanted to know its history. If he had the time he would tell them about the secret cupboard and the letter he and Emily had found.

This couple were different. The shop was quiet enough so she could hear them talking and the pair were seriously interested in buying the desk.

Emily's heart pounded. She knew the sale would be extremely good for the shop but she felt as if it were her desk. She knew she hadn't bought it but it was hers in every other way.

'Would we be able to pay for it in instalments?' asked the girl.

'I'm afraid not,' said Cameron. 'I can only accept full payment.'

'Would you take an offer?' she asked.

'Again, I'm afraid not. If you Google antique oak writing desks you'll see that this price is in line with what they sell for whenever they become available. Of course, given the desk's age, that doesn't happen very often.'

Emily let out a breath she hadn't realised she was holding as the couple thanked Cameron for his time and left.

Cameron turned round and grinned at Emily.

'I think we've sold the desk.'

'But they left.'

'I know, but they'll be back. They've already pictured it in their house. They just need to go away and justify spending that amount of money on a desk. See,' he said, turning back to the desk, 'they're staring at it through the window. She really wants it.'

'Oh,' said Emily, 'That's good . . . '

'Hey, what's wrong?'

'Nothing,' said Emily, suddenly very busy with some paperwork by the till.

'Yes there is. Your face has gone all flat.'

'Flat?'

'Yeah, it's the look you get when something's upset you. What is it?'

Emily shrugged. He was being ridiculous. How can a face look flat?

'Is it the desk?'

'There's nothing wrong,' said Emily, her voice rising in exasperation.

'It's the desk. You're upset because someone wants to buy it.'

She shrugged again. 'Maybe a little bit.'

She waited for him to laugh at her. This was a shop, everything here was for sale. It was crazy to get attached to a writing desk for which she didn't even have any use.

'What I said to the couple isn't true,' he said. 'If *you* want to buy it you can have it for the money it cost me.'

She looked up at him. He wasn't laughing. That was a really generous offer considering how much the shop needed the profit.

She walked over to the desk and ran a hand over its surface. She loved the rich feel of the wood under her fingers. She loved its mystery and its clever little hidey-holes. She even liked its old musty smell that spoke to her of bygone intrigues.

'Thank you, that's a really kind offer but I've not got a home to put it in,' she said. 'And I'd probably find it hard to carry it to New Zealand.'

She'd meant it as a joke but he didn't laugh.

'So you're definitely going then?'

She looked at him in surprise.

They'd talked about her trip so many times. She'd booked flights, not only to New Zealand but to the three countries she was going to afterwards. Of course she was going, he knew that . . . and then she knew . . .

'Don't tell me you've been talking to Dad and he's told you he doesn't think I'm capable of going?'

The words came out harsher than she'd intended. It wasn't his fault her parents were trying to manage her life — but he should have known better than to listen to them. He was supposed to be her friend.

'I've not spoken to Tom about your trip once.'

'Mum told you his concerns then.'

He blushed slightly at being caught out and then he sighed.

'Maddie mentioned something the other day about them being worried about you.' He held up a hand to stop her from saying anything. 'And before you get huffy it's perfectly natural for parents to worry about their only child going off around the world on her own. And,' he held up his hand again as she was about to argue, 'I know you're all grown up but you'll always be their baby, so just accept their worrying as a part of life and move on.'

He was right of course and to snap at him after he'd been so generous was rude.

'Sorry,' she said. 'I'm just a bit irritated by them interfering even though I know they're only trying to help. I'm being driven insane, what with Mum and that dreadful party and the endless stream of eligible bachelors, and Dad with his silent panicking about this trip.'

Cameron's lips twitched.

'How do you spot silent panicking?'

Emily laughed. Trust Cameron to find levity in the situation.

'He doesn't talk when I mention anything to do with travelling and then he goes out into the garden and spends several hours doing very intense gardening.'

'Call me next time. I'd like to see what intense gardening looks like.'

She laughed.

'Can I go out for lunch now?'

'Will you grab a sandwich for me while you're out?' he asked.

'Don't you want to take a lunch break?'

'Emily, for the first time in a long time the shop has a steady stream of customers. I want to make the most of it.'

So she left him to it. As she walked away from the shop she saw the couple from earlier returning. Cameron had been right — he had made a sale.

She forced herself to walk briskly away from the shop. No one got teary about a desk — no one.

When she returned an hour later, laden down with a new travel backpack and some guidebooks to places she was going to visit, as well as lunch for Cameron, there was a large Sold sticker on the desk.

12

Emily had slumped down in the passenger seat so only the top of her hair was visible from outside the car.

'What are you doing?' hissed Cameron.

'I'm hiding,' said Emily.

'Why?' he asked as they drove slowly down the country lane.

'I don't want Paul Standen to see me as we drive past. He might recognise me and hide somewhere and then this drive will have been a wasted journey.'

'But he'll see me.'

'You're on the other side of the car; you'll be much harder to make out.'

Cameron grinned. She was acting like a TV detective again, but not a particularly good one.

'But he'll spot my car so we won't be able to use it again. We'll have to steal a replacement.'

'Let's make sure we steal one with air conditioning,' muttered Emily.

They turned round a sharp bend and started on the steep journey down into Lentworth's town centre. Cameron could just make out Paul Standen's cottage about halfway down the hill.

'Are you dissing my car?' he asked.

Emily laughed and said, 'You can't use words like 'dissing', you're too old.'

Cameron took in a huge breath of mock outrage. 'How dare you! You should get out and walk for that major insult.' The car followed a curve in the road. 'Ah, best not get out here, his house is coming up on the left.'

They sat in silence as he drove past the house.

'Was he in his garden?' Emily whispered once they were past.

Cameron burst out laughing and said, 'Sit up, you crazy girl, and stop whispering! I couldn't see him in his garden but that doesn't mean he wasn't there. Even more flowers have opened up since we were last here and it was difficult to see even the front of his house.'

She sat up as they turned round another bend — and there was Paul Standen, walking towards them. Emily ducked again as Cameron laughed.

Paul Standen was making slow, painful progress up the hill and didn't even look at the car as Cameron drove past.

When they reached the town, Cameron pulled into a small car park near the high street and stopped the car under a shady tree.

'You've gone very serious all of a sudden,' said Emily.

'He's an old man, Emily. I'm not sure we should be bothering him. Is it really worth causing him stress at this stage of his life?'

'It's not like we're going to be aggressive,' said Emily. 'If he doesn't want to talk we'll leave.'

'Hmm,' said Cameron, 'I'm not sure we should approach him. He looked so frail just now.'

She nodded.

'OK, we'll head into the town and ask around, but if no one knows anything please can we try him? I promise I'll be gentle. I don't want to be responsible for causing an old man any stress either.'

'Well, OK then.'

Cameron pulled down the sun visor to check the bruise on his cheek. It was fading but it still looked as if he'd been in a fight.

'Don't worry about it,' she said, catching what he was doing. 'You look as gorgeous as ever.'

She opened her door and stepped out.

Did she really think he was gorgeous or was she being facetious? If she thought he was good-looking, did that mean . . . ? No, he wasn't going to go there. No point giving himself false hopes.

He looked at his bruise again and smiled. Acting the idiot at the beach the other day had been worth it to hear her peals of laughter. She'd laughed so hard and looked so carefree and young that he would have gone on falling off the board all day, even if he had accidentally flipped the board and hit himself in the face.

After the paddle boarding Emily had gone home and the rest of them had gone for a late Sunday lunch. His friends had been remorseless in their teasing. At least they'd listened to him and not made any innuendos while Emily had been around but after she'd gone they didn't let up.

'Because,' said his friend Louisa, when he'd asked them why, 'we've not seen you so interested in a girl for a very, very long time.'

'She's just a friend.'

His friends had all laughed.

'Cam,' said Louisa, 'when we speak to you, it's all Emily this and Emily that. Earlier on, you couldn't take your eyes off her for more than a few seconds. And that falling off the board thing to make her laugh . . . mate, you're besotted!'

He'd denied it, of course, but that

didn't stop them going on and on about it.

Looking at her now, standing outside the car waiting for him to join her, he tried to be objective.

She was wearing a pale yellow summer dress that clung to her slender frame and finished just above her knees. Her arms were bare and tanned by the sun and on her shoulders was a faint smattering of freckles. He couldn't see her face but he knew that her green eyes would be serious even while her mouth would be waiting for a reason to smile. Her blonde hair was loose and it hung down her back to her shoulder blades.

Yes, she was beautiful but there were plenty of beautiful women about, so what was it about her that was making it so difficult for him to look at another woman? He thought about her intelligence and humour, her loyalty and her passion and then he thought he'd be better off creating a list of reasons why he shouldn't fall in love with her. It would be better for his mental health if he stayed clear of that disaster!

He got out of the car.

'Where do you want to start?' he asked.

'Let's wander down the high street,' she said. 'If we go into the boutique shops — the owners are far more likely to know the locals. Hopefully we'll get lucky.'

He stifled a sigh; this was going to be a boring morning.

★ ★ ★

Two hours later Cameron stopped suddenly outside a café.

'What is it?' asked Emily.

'I'm not going any further until I've had something to eat,' he said.

'Good idea, I'm starving.'

'You're always starving,' he said, pushing open the café door and holding it open for her.

'That's true,' she said, 'but I'm even more starving than normal. This detective business is hard work.'

'And boring.'

'That is also true,' she said as she pulled out a chair and flopped onto it. 'We're not getting anywhere, are we?'

'Well, you got a sun hat and I got a magazine but otherwise, no. We are doing very badly.'

'All roads keep leading back to Paul Standen.'

His had been the only name to come up in relation to Dottie. If anyone had anything to say, and most people didn't, it was that he was the only person they could think of who might know something.

It would seem he was the only one left alive from that era. Everyone else in the town was either too young to have been alive at the same time as Harry Logan or had never been around Logan Hall at the time he'd been alive.

'Fine,' said Cameron, his good intentions scattered to the wind after the last two boring hours. 'We'll eat and then go and call on him.'

Emily smiled and picked up a menu. 'I'll get this,' she said, 'as a thank you for driving me here, yet again.'

He didn't argue. Even though his cash flow had improved slightly over the last week, he still owed a considerable amount of money to the bank. If things in the shop continued to improve in the way they had over the last week, he'd eventually be able to spend money without worrying — in about five years' time!

He hadn't said anything to Emily yet but he had a possible solution to the Devon problem. He was wary of telling her because he knew she'd jump at the opportunity and he wasn't convinced it was a good idea. It would cost him, both financially and emotionally.

Emily came back to the table with two crusty filled baguettes and a bowl of chips to share. Cameron tucked in immediately but Emily pulled a Home To Home flyer and a pen out of her handbag. She turned the flyer over and started to write on it.

'What are you doing?' he asked.

'I'm going to write Paul Standen a

note explaining what we're doing and that the only thing we want from him is an address for Dottie. He can ring the shop or he can contact me on my mobile if he has any information.'

She was being incredibly optimistic. If Paul Standen wouldn't talk to them when they were outside his house it was unlikely he was going to ring them for a chat, but Cameron didn't want to rain on her parade so he let her carry on.

He had made serious inroads into the bowl of chips by the time she had finished writing her note. She folded the paper and put it carefully into her handbag.

'Thanks for coming along with me today,' she said. 'I know this whole business doesn't interest you that much but it's important to me.'

Cameron looked at her for a moment. Should he confess he came along because he wanted to spend as much time with her as possible before she left? No, that was probably a very bad idea.

Instead he said, 'It's important to me because it's important to you.'

She smiled and then, before he could stop her, she emptied the remaining chips onto her plate.

'Hey,' he said, 'I thought those were to share.'

'They were, which is why I've put a lot less than half on my plate. The rest are in your stomach.'

'I didn't eat that many.'

'Yes, you did,' she said and she popped a small, crunchy chip into her mouth.

He reached over and swiped another one from her plate. The chips were too good to be polite!

After lunch, they decided to leave his car where he'd parked it that morning and to walk up the hill to Paul Standen's house.

Their first walk up this hill a few weeks ago had been filled with a tortuous silence but this time couldn't be more different. Cameron found himself talking a lot about himself and his life before the shop. He even discussed his childhood — not about his parents' painful divorce but about moving to Brighton afterwards.

'My accent was so strong,' he said, 'most people couldn't understand me.'

'It's only very faint now. What happened?'

'Well, at first I thought everyone was stupid down South.' Emily laughed. 'But then I realised I was talking too fast with too strong an accent. When I slowed down I was finally able to get fed and clothed and everything improved from there. I guess I lost my accent the longer I stayed here.'

'Do you miss Scotland?'

'I miss the people most. My grand-parents are still there, and then there's my mother. Edinburgh is an amazing, vibrant city so I always enjoy a visit. But I was young when I left and so my roots are in Brighton. How about you?'

'How about me, what?'

'Where are your roots?'

'That's a difficult question. My

parents have lived in that house since before I was born so I guess my roots are there, but I loved living in London, felt I belonged there.'

'Really? Didn't you find it too hectic?'

'Yes, but that's part of the fun of it. All those people from different cultures mixing together, working alongside each other, it made me feel connected to a vast network. Then there's the history. Not only do I feel like I'm walking in the footsteps of hundreds of years of history I also feel like I'm part of it, like I'm adding to the greatness of the place, like everyone who lives and works there. Having said all that, I don't think I'll live in London again.'

'Really? You almost had me sold on the idea of moving there.'

'I'd miss the sea too much. So I guess I'm like you — my roots are in Brighton.'

That was good news, Cameron thought. It meant even if she went away she was likely to return. How long would it take before she came home, though?

They had reached their destination and, outside Paul Standen's garden Emily put her hand on his garden gate but she didn't push it open.

'What's wrong?' Cameron asked.

'I'm nervous . . . '

He put his hand on hers. 'We've come this far,' he said. 'We've only got to go a few more yards and then we might get some answers.'

She pushed the gate open. Paul Standen's cottage garden was a riot of colour with no lawn in sight and every conceivable piece of ground surrounding the narrow path to the house was covered in flowers of different sizes. It was chaotically wonderful!

Cameron looked towards the vegetable patch but there was no sign of Paul anywhere.

Emily knocked on the front door and waited. There was no sound from the house. She tried again and this time Cameron thought he saw movement through one of the front windows, but when he looked again everything was still.

They waited.

'Oh well,' said Emily when nothing happened, 'At least we tried.' She pushed her note through the letterbox, 'I suppose we should just go now?'

Cameron pulled her towards him and gave her a strong hug followed by a brotherly kiss on the forehead. 'I'm sorry, Emily,' he said 'But I think we've done all we can do here. Let's go home.'

She nodded and allowed herself to be led out of the garden.

She was quiet on the walk back to the car and as she walked in front of him and he could see from the way she held herself that she was feeling defeated. He didn't like to see her looking like that.

'I've had an idea,' he said, unable to stand it any longer. 'I've a friend who lives in Devon. We could go and stay with Alex next weekend and visit the last known address we have for Dottie.'

He hadn't meant to ask her. It would mean a whole weekend away from the shop at a time when it needed all his attention. And it would cost him — not money, as Alex would put them up for free — but he was perilously close to falling in love with Emily . . .

A weekend away with her, when they didn't have work to come between them, might tip him over the edge — and he knew that then there would be no going back . . .

13

Maddie pulled Emily's faded blue jeans out of her suitcase. 'You can't take these!'

'Yes I can, Mum, they're comfy.'

Emily went to grab them back but her mother was surprisingly nimble and danced out of reach.

'Darling, they do nothing for you.' Maddie dodged past Emily and opened her wardrobe. 'How about this skirt instead?'

'That's a work skirt, Mum. I'd feel like I was going for a job interview. Let me pack in peace.'

Emily managed to get her jeans back and repacked them, much to Maddie's disgust.

'They're scruffy, Emily. You can't make all this effort to hunt for this woman and then turn up looking like a vagabond!' Maddie was still standing at

Emily's wardrobe looking at each item of clothing in turn. 'How about this?' she asked, pulling out a maxi dress.

The dress was one of Emily's favourites. Normally maxi dresses swamped her tiny frame but this one had been made especially for petite people. It was dark blue with two coloured panels running from underneath the arm to the hem at the bottom of the dress. It came in underneath the chest and the cut gave the illusion that she had a waist.

'OK, I'll take that one.'

Triumphant, Maddie handed Emily the dress for her to put it in the suitcase. There was no way Maddie was moving and giving up her position of power by the wardrobe!

'This one's very nice,' she added.

'Mum, I haven't worn that since my university days. It's indecently short. Now put it back.'

'Everyone should have a little black dress.'

'Which is why I've never thrown it out but I'm not taking it to Devon with me. It's not like we'll be going out clubbing.'

'What if Cameron and you go out for dinner?'

'We're staying with his friend, Alex, so I doubt we'll be going out for meals together. If we do go out for dinner I'm far more likely to wear my comfy jeans than a little black dress that's far too short for someone of my age.'

'Oh, but you mustn't wear those jeans if you go out for dinner, Emily — I'll disown you! There must be something more suitable in here,' she said and resumed her hunt through Emily's wardrobe. 'Ah, this is perfect.' She pulled out a pale blue dress that Emily had recently bought in a sale. It had a v-neckline with a tight fitting bodice and a flared skirt. It was perfect for this weather so even though it was a little on the dressy side Emily allowed her mother to put it in the suitcase.

'I think that's enough now, Mum,' she said as Maddie went back to the wardrobe. 'We're only going away for one night. I don't even need one change of clothes let alone more than two.'

'You must be prepared for every eventuality,' said Maddie as she pulled out another dress.

A horrible thought dawned on Emily.

'Mum,' she said, 'you *do* know this isn't a date weekend, don't you?'

Maddie said nothing, but continued to rifle through Emily's wardrobe, not looking at Emily.

'Mum,' she said, her tone a low warning.

'Oh, Emily,' Maddie finally replied. 'What would be so wrong with having a little fun with him?'

'I am having fun with him, Mum — just not in the sense you mean.'

Maddie took her daughter's hand and led her over to the bed. It looked like she was in for another heart-to-heart. She suppressed a sigh. She had loads to be getting on with and she could do without this.

'But why not in the way I mean? He's

very good-looking — at least I think so. I mean those eyes, they're so brown, like polished walnut!'

'Polished walnut? That's an odd description. Most people would say like melted chocolate.'

'I don't know why people say that. Melted chocolate is very sludgy-looking. Anyway, that's beside the point. He's handsome, he makes you laugh, you enjoy his company . . . and *he* clearly, well, he clearly . . . '

'Clearly, what, Mum?'

'Well, he clearly cares for you.'

How typical of her mum to misinterpret what was going on between her and Cameron!

They were friends, that was all, nothing else. Cameron had lots of female friends — she'd met a handful of them the other day. He was obviously close to them with no other agenda than to hang out and have fun.

She wasn't any different.

'I agree with you that he's very good-looking, but before you get all excited, I should stress that there is nothing going on between me and Cameron. And if you're suggesting that I go away and have a wild weekend with him before I leave for New Zealand next week, then I'll remind you that goes against everything you brought me up to believe, doesn't it now, Mum?

'Plus — and this is the most important point — it doesn't matter how amazing Cameron is, I made a promise to Johnny and I have no intention of breaking it.'

'What promise, darling?' said Maddie softly.

'I promised him there would be no one else.'

'Oh love,' said Maddie, a tear running down her face. 'Did he ask you to make this promise?'

'No, but . . . '

'And was he aware you made this promise?'

'No, but . . . '

'Oh Emily! You know Johnny would never have asked something like that of you. He would have wanted you to find someone else, to be happy. Johnny was always about living in the moment and enjoying life to the full. He wouldn't want you to live life like a nun.'

'I know, Mum,' said Emily, pulling her hands out from underneath her mother's and walking over to the window. 'But he's not here to give me his opinion on anything, is he? And that's the crucial point in all this. Johnny is not here.'

Maddie stood and wiped the tears from her face with the back of her hand.

'OK, love. I'll leave you to pack in peace, then, shall I?'

Emily nodded, not trusting herself to speak. She hated to see her mother upset and she wanted to say something to make the situation right but she couldn't say what she wanted to hear.

For a long time after Maddie had left the room Emily stood at her bedroom window looking out at one of her favourite views.

From her vantage point, high up in the attic, she could see the English Channel over the rooftops of the houses stretching out into the distance. She'd always found it soothing to stand here and watch the water. It was timeless. To the left, she could see Brighton pier jutting out into the sea and on a good day she could make out some of the rides.

She smiled as she saw the Booster slowly begin to turn before speeding up and spinning its riders round and round. Cameron had been so funny on that ride, trying and failing to put a brave front on something he clearly found terrifying.

Her mother was right; he was all of the great things she'd listed and more. In a different lifetime they could have had a fantastic life together with lots of laughter. She could actually picture it. But this wasn't a different lifetime and it was never going to happen.

After a while Emily pulled the suitcase off her bed and dumped it on the floor. She was tired and they had an early start tomorrow to get to Devon. It was too hot to get under the covers so she lay on top of the duvet and stared at the ceiling. It took a long time for sleep to come.

* * *

Emily woke at five and knew she wouldn't get back to sleep. She'd never been a late sleeper but as she'd grown older she found it difficult to sleep past six. She'd tried lying in bed to see if she'd drop off again but it never happened.

She got up quietly and had a quick shower, trying not to disturb her parents.

When she was done she poured herself a bowl of cereal and took it outside to eat. She loved the peace and quiet of early mornings, especially in the summer when she could sit outside and listen to the birds singing.

This morning she wasn't alone in the garden.

Her father was sitting in one of the wicker chairs, a mug of coffee in one hand and his empty cereal bowl on the table in front of him.

'Hello, Dad,' she said.

They sat in silence while Emily ate her cereal. Tom wasn't much of a talker — he didn't need to be because Maddie did enough talking for both of them! — but he was a solid, dependable presence and when he did speak everyone listened.

This morning he stood, picked up his bowl and made to go past Emily. Just as he'd reached her chair, he stopped. He laid his hand on her shoulder and said, 'You're my greatest joy, Emily. Don't rule out having children of your own.'

Not waiting for a response he gave her shoulder a squeeze and walked into the house.

Emily puffed out her cheeks and then slowly released the air in one long breath. Then she picked up her breakfast things and followed her father into the house. He wasn't in the kitchen and his breakfast things had been cleared away. There was no evidence that the encounter in the garden had happened at all — but the whole thing had left her feeling winded.

She glanced at the clock; it was just after six. Cameron had said they would leave at seven to avoid the holiday traffic heading into Devon on the M5. She had a whole hour to spare and she didn't want to spend it dwelling on what her father had said.

She'd been putting off emailing a few of her university friends who were trying to organise a reunion. It was the last thing she wanted to go to without Johnny so she was glad she had the excuse of not being in the country. She'd email them now and break the news.

Opening her inbox, she found an email from Don, her old boss. After the embarrassment of her mother's party she'd found the courage to email him and ask if there were any jobs available in the States. He'd not responded and as the weeks had passed she'd almost forgotten about it. After all, it had been an impulsive email born out of frustration.

She almost didn't want to open his response but after all this time, surely he was only going to tell her it wasn't possible.

She clicked it open.

Emily

How good to hear from you! I trust you're well and enjoying this fabulous summer.

I'm delighted that you want to come back to us. Your talents have been sorely missed by everyone.

Now for the good news . . .

Do you remember Kate Williams? She remembers you. She's been asked to head up a new team to put together a project (details below) based in the States. It's a two-year contract with the possibility of an extension. I mentioned your name to her and she was thrilled at the idea of having you in her team!

I understand from your email that you're going travelling for several months, starting next week, so if you are interested we'll have to move quickly.

Please read the job description below and email me back ASAP. If you're keen, we'll arrange a Skype meeting for you to chat to Kate about the details.

Lovely to hear from you, Emily.

Don

She read through the job description and then, because she couldn't quite believe her eyes, read it through again. It was perfect! It was everything she'd enjoyed about her old job and more. She'd be a fool not to go for it.

Her fingers hovered over the reply button.

Was there any reason not to do this?

She felt a tiny pang in her heart when she thought about the job she'd be leaving behind. How would Cameron cope without her?

That was a silly worry, she told herself firmly. After all, he knew she was going away anyway, and he would need to find someone to replace her — which shouldn't be difficult.

She hit the reply button.

14

Trucks thundered past Emily's open window and Cameron's car shuddered. 'Please can you wind up your window?' he pleaded.

'We'll die from overheating!' Emily argued — *not to mention poisoning by that terrible sock smell!* — which Emily didn't say because Cameron was doing her a huge favour.

'Every time a truck goes past it makes me jump. If I swerve and hit another car it will be a much quicker death than slowly dying through heat exhaustion.'

Emily wound her window up nearly all the way.

'Is that any better?' she asked.

'I guess so . . . '

She turned away from him and looked out of her window. It turned out Cameron was a tense and tetchy driver on the motorway. She smiled. Who would've guessed it?

She had suggested they travel on the A303 avoiding motorways altogether but he was having none of it.

'I've been down to Devon that way before and it's a nightmare,' he'd said. 'If we stick to the motorway at least we'll be on fast roads.'

She hadn't been in a position to argue with him — she wasn't doing the driving after all — but it did mean that the window had been a source of tension since they'd hit the M25. The M5 was even worse as the day became hotter and the sheer volume of traffic slowed them down.

'There's a service station coming up in a few miles,' said Cameron. 'Let's stop there for something to eat.'

Emily didn't need to be asked twice; she was going to down at least two litres of water and lie in the shade for half an hour! He had barely switched off the engine before she was out of the car and stretching her legs.

He wasn't far behind her.

'That was horrendous,' he said, reverting back to his normal self as soon as they were out of the car.

'Absolutely awful,' she agreed.

'We still have another hour and a half to go until we get to Alex's house.'

'Let's get some water and something to eat,' she said. 'Hopefully that will make us feel a little more human.'

They traipsed into the service station. It was soulless inside but at least it was blessedly cool.

'Find us a table,' said Emily, 'and I'll get the food. Is pizza OK?'

'It's more than OK. Don't forget the water.'

'I'll bring as much as I can carry.'

Emily chose two large pizzas, one loaded with meat for Cameron and a sweet chilli chicken one for herself. She also brought four bottles of water.

Cameron had chosen a seat by the window but he leapt up when he saw her coming.

'Here, let me carry that.' He took the

heavy tray out her hands and carried it back to the plastic chairs.

'Wow,' he said, when he clocked the food, 'Are we expecting guests?'

She laughed. 'I asked for large but I wasn't expecting them to be *this* big. We can always wrap what we don't eat in some napkins and save it for later.'

Cameron emptied one bottle of water before he attacked the pizza with a vengeance.

Despite ordering a large pizza, Emily wasn't that hungry. She hadn't been since she'd emailed Don that morning. She looked in her handbag, wanting to check her phone to see if he'd replied.

'Damn,' she murmured.

'What's wrong?' asked Cameron around a mouthful of pizza.

'I've left my phone in the car.'

'Do you need it?'

'Well, I'm waiting for an email from my old boss. He wanted me to get back to him about something quickly, which I did. I know it's a Saturday but Don's never far away from his emails so I'm waiting for a response.'

'Is it important?' asked Cameron, putting down his pizza and making to get up to fetch it.

'It can wait,' said Emily.

'Sure?'

She nodded as she took a bite of her pizza. She found she was reluctant to tell him about the potential job in the States, although she wasn't sure why. She ought to tell him — there was nothing to hide.

'I've asked him about getting a job as a computer programmer,' she eventually said. 'It's about time I went back to it.'

'That's great news.' He looked really pleased, more pleased than she expected. 'What did he want you to get back to him quickly about? Is there a job available?'

'There is. They want me to have a chat with them about it as soon as possible . . . well, they said 'chat' but they mean interview. Although I think they're pretty keen for me to go back.

They didn't want me to leave in the first place.'

'Of course you'll get the job. If you're even half as good as a computer programmer as you are an underpaid shop assistant then you must be amazing. When does the job start?'

'The project would start in about six months.'

'That's perfect for you. It means you could still get all your travelling in and then have a job to come back to,' Cameron enthused.

'Ah . . . ' she said hesistantly. 'The thing is . . . well, the exciting bit is that the job is in America.'

'Oh . . . ' Cameron's expression changed dramatically and he put his pizza back on his plate. 'For how long?'

'It's only a temporary position.' She couldn't bring herself to tell him it was for at least two years, if not longer.

'Oh, I see . . . well, that's great, I suppose. I hope the interview goes well.'

He picked up his pizza and started

eating it again, but this time with a lot less gusto. He seemed to be preoccupied with something going on outside the window but when she looked in that direction all she could see were cars pulling in and out of the spaces.

They ate the rest of their lunch in silence.

For once the amount of food beat Emily and she wrapped her remaining pizza in a napkin. They bought some more water for the journey and left the service station.

The next few miles passed in silence. Cameron didn't even gripe when she wound her window down fully.

'Did you check your phone?' he asked, as they came off the M5 an hour later.

'No,' she said. 'I forgot.'

Faced with Cameron's quietness she'd lost some of her enthusiasm. She rooted around in the glove box and pulled the phone out. There were no emails but there was a missed call.

'Are you going to call it back?' Cameron asked when she told him.

'But I don't know who it is,' she said. 'It's not a London area code.'

'Why don't you Google the number? It's probably a cold caller. You can block it if it is.'

She typed the number in and gasped.

'What is it?'he asked.

'It doesn't say who called but the area code is for Lentworth — and there's only one person living there who has my number.'

He glanced across at her. 'Paul Standen. Call him back,' he said.

She pressed call and waited. Nothing. She looked at her phone. 'I don't believe it. No signal.'

'Keep an eye on it. We're bound to go through an area with signal soon. I can pull over so you don't lose him.'

For the rest of the journey she kept one eye on her phone and the other one on the road, but nothing changed.

'I'm sure Alex will have a landline,' said Cameron, 'so you can make the call to that if needs be.'

She nodded, frustrated at getting so

close to talking to him only to be thwarted by technology.

'We're nearly there,' said Cameron.

'Does Alex live in the town of Paignton?'

'No, the house is about a mile-and-a-half out of town. I think you'll love it there. All the rooms at the back of the house have a view of the sea and the lounge doors open out onto a private terrace. You can walk from the terrace down onto the National Coastal Path. It's a dream location really. Alex was very lucky to inherit the property.'

'Do you visit often?'

'I used to, but this is my first time for a while.'

They drove down an unremarkable street and pulled up in front of a whitewashed, three-storey house. It was pleasant enough to look at but she could see nothing special about it.

He smiled at her. 'Let's go meet Alex, freshen up, and then we can head out to the farm.'

Right now the last thing she wanted

to do was get back into the car and do more driving but if they didn't get to the farm this afternoon they'd have no time to track down Dottie tomorrow.

They got out of the car just as the front door opened.

'Cam,' said a tall, dark-haired woman, 'you're here!'

'Hi, Alex.' He walked over to greet her.

Alex was a woman?

Why hadn't Emily realised that? And of course she was beautiful — with slender legs that went on for miles and long, thick dark hair. Emily had never seen her level of gorgeousness outside a magazine. Suddenly Emily was convinced that she looked even more sweaty and crumpled than she already felt!

Alex wrapped her arms around Cameron's neck and held him close — rather closer than a friend would, and for longer, too. So this was another one of Cameron's exes? Emily didn't know why she was so shocked — the country must be littered with them!

Alex finally let Cameron go and turned her bewitching smile on Emily.

'You must be Emily,' she said. 'It's so nice to meet you. You've done such amazing things with Cam's website. You're a genius to be able to persuade this Luddite to do that.'

Alex shook Emily's hand warmly and then kissed her briefly on the cheek. Emily had a whiff of a delicious floral scent before Alex stepped back and said, 'You both must be exhausted. Come into the house and freshen up before you head off again.'

Cameron pulled both suitcases out of his boot and, refusing Emily's offer to carry her own, dragged them up the driveway to the front door.

Inside Alex's house was cool and beautifully decorated. Cameron's influence could be seen everywhere in the choice of furniture.

Emily spotted a photograph frame that looked like one of Cameron's creations. Their relationship must have lasted more than Cameron's norm of a few weeks.

Emily's tummy started to feel strangely twisted and fluttery.

'Are you all right?' Alex had noticed, her voice full of concern.

'My stomach feels a bit strange,' she confessed. 'It must be from all that sitting down in the heat of the car.'

'You poor thing,' said Alex. 'Do you think a shower might help or would you prefer something to drink first?'

Emily wanted to be alone for a bit.

'A shower would be great,' she said.

'Cam, I've put Emily in the room at the top of the house. Could you take her suitcase up?'

To Emily she said, 'That room has a little en-suite and when I say little, I mean tiny, but it should do the job. Do you like real lemonade? I've got some chilling so we could have that with some ice after you've freshened up and before you set out again.'

Having assured her hostess she loved real lemonade, Emily followed Cameron to the third floor. The guest room was decorated in light colours with white bed linen, but what caught Emily's attention was the view from the window. From her vantage point up high she could see the sea stretching out for miles with no houses blocking any part of the view. Gulls dived for food and white sail boats bobbed on the water. It was a view Emily could watch for hours.

'I told you you'd love it,' said Cameron and Emily realised he was standing very close to her watching her reaction.

She stepped away from him.

'Thanks for bringing my case up,' she said briskly. 'I'll take a shower, then I'll come down and join you two.'

'OK — if you need anything just shout. I'm in the room directly below.'

Was he sharing with Alex? She didn't want to know. It was none of her business, anyway.

As promised, the bathroom was tiny but the space was utilised ingeniously.

She stepped into the shower and turned the water to cool. It was blissful.

For a few moments she forgot about Don, about Alex and Cameron, and even Dottie and just enjoyed the feeling of cool water running all over her.

There was a fluffy white towel hanging on the back of the bathroom door and she wrapped it around herself when she'd finished.

She unzipped her suitcase and pulled out her pale blue summer dress, grateful to her mother for insisting she pack it. She shook it out. It was a little crumpled but it was better than the outfit she'd had on when she arrived. Wearing it, she wouldn't feel quite such a frump next to the gorgeous Alex.

She slipped on low-heeled sandals, brushed her hair and then checked her reflection. She was too pale; next to the naturally tanned Alex she would look ill. She opened her make-up bag and ran a light dusting of bronzer over her cheeks. She was about to put on lipstick but decided against it. She didn't wear it normally so Cameron would notice. He might wonder why she'd put it on

— and she wasn't sure what the answer to that really was.

Surely she wasn't jealous of Alex. There was no reason for her to be. She dropped the lipstick back in her make-up bag. She'd do as she was.

She was about to go downstairs when she remembered to check her phone. She had a signal. She was so pleased she did a little dance of joy and then rang the mysterious number.

It rang and rang. She was just about to put the phone down when somebody answered.

'Hello,' said a gruff voice.

'Hello, this is Emily Robson. You rang me earlier but I didn't get to the phone in time.'

'Is this the girl from the furniture shop?'

'Yes.'

'It's Paul Standen here. You want to know if I've an address for Dottie.'

'Yes, please.'

'Well, I haven't.'

Emily felt a wave of crushing

disappointment and she sank down on the bed.

'Oh, I see. Well, thank you for phoning me anyway,' she said.

'Are you still looking for her?'

'Yes.'

'Well, I've a message for her if you find her.'

'OK.'

'Tell her I'm sorry.'

'Oh . . . will she know what for?'

There was silence. It lasted a full minute and Emily was beginning to wonder if he'd put the phone down on her.

Then he said, 'No, she won't know what for.'

Emily waited for a moment. This was one of the strangest telephone conversations she'd ever had!

'All right, I suppose I should tell you what I did,' Standen said at last. 'I only ever told my Meredith this story before but I don't suppose there's any harm in telling you now.

'See, I was a silly boy who thought I was a man when I met Dottie Smith. I knew of her before that, of course — Lentworth is a small place — but she was younger than me so we didn't mix with the same people.

'I knew what she looked like — she was hard to miss. She could really turn a boy's head, could Dottie, she was that beautiful. She was funny as well, and when I realised she was interested in me . . . well, I was that made up. We'd only been walking out a few weeks when we both got jobs at Logan Hall. Me as a junior gardener, her as a maid. We thought we were so grown-up.

'I had it all planned out, see . . . me and my beautiful girl in a cottage surrounded by flowers, raising our children. It took me years to see that Dottie wouldn't have been satisfied with that life. She was destined for greater things, was Dottie.'

Paul Standen coughed and Emily shuffled back on the bed until she was leaning on the pillows.

'I was there when Harry and Dottie met, and I saw then and there that my dream was never going to happen. He was mesmerised by her, you see. Wherever she went around that huge house he would follow.

'He was a good-looking chap too, and he'd had the benefit of a good education. I tried to stop it happening but my words came out spiteful when they should have been loving. She very quickly stopped walking out with me and not long after that she started walking out with him instead.

'I don't blame her; I wouldn't have wanted to spend time with me either. But I did blame them both at the time. I was so angry. I tried to be civil because I didn't want to be out of her life completely — which I would have been, had I voiced my feelings. Quite honestly most of the time I wanted to punch the blighter in the face! He had everything I didn't. Ah, what an awful thing jealousy is.'

Emily heard Paul take a deep breath and then he sighed it back out again.

'What I did was a spiteful thing. I feel

guilty about it even today, seventy years later.

'He gave her that letter and necklace you found just before he went away to war. I found it one day when I was snooping where I shouldn't and I hid it in that desk of yours. Dottie was distraught that she'd lost it but I thought it served them right.

'When he died . . . well, I went to that funeral and I saw how devastated she was and I knew then what a horrible thing I'd done, but I couldn't make it right.'

Paul Standen went quiet again.

After a moment, Emily said quietly, 'Thank you, Mr Standen, for ringing me and telling me your story. I'm glad you felt able to do so.'

'That's all right, lass. I hope you find her and return that necklace.'

'Mr Standen, I really don't think you need to feel guilty about something you did when you were so young.'

Paul Standen let out a snort of laughter.

'Thank you, lass. That's what my Meredith said, but I do feel guilty, you see, because in the end I did get my dream. I met Meredith, my true, gorgeous girl and we raised our children with that beautiful garden all around us. But poor Harry Logan, he died on some battlefield when he was only twenty-four.'

'That wasn't your fault, Mr Standen.'

'True enough, lass. Well, if you do find her, give her my apologies. Goodbye now.'

And with that he was gone and Emily didn't know whether to laugh or cry.

Poor Dottie — her love gone and her only memento of him consigned to a hidden cupboard. Yet she didn't blame Paul Standen. He'd also lost someone he loved through no fault of his own.

She popped her phone back into her handbag and headed downstairs, where she found Alex putting some drinks on a tray. Cameron was nowhere to be seen.

'Shall we sit outside while we wait for

Cam?' Alex asked.

'That would be lovely,' she said, although thinking it would be anything but. What could she say to this lovely woman whose relationship to Cameron was as yet undefined?

She followed Alex out on to the terrace and they sat on some cushioned wicker seats.

A gentle sea breeze cooled them and Emily scrabbled for something to talk to her about. There were so many things she didn't want to discuss, both of their relationships with Cameron being top of the list. It was Alex who initiated the conversation by asking her about her dress and soon the two of them were discussing their favourite places to shop.

'Hey,' said Cameron when he came out to join them. He was freshly showered with his damp hair curling around his ears. He was wearing a pale green T-shirt that flattered his muscles. Emily caught Alex gazing at him before she seemed to shake herself and offer him a drink.

'Thanks,' he said, 'but we'd better be going.'

Once they were folded back into Cameron's cramped car Emily told him all about Paul Standen's phone call.

'He was really very sweet after all,' she said when she'd finished the story.

'Sweet? Do you really think so?'

'Well, yes. Don't you?'

'He hid the poor girl's letter in a secret cupboard because he was angry that she'd chosen someone else. He had more than one opportunity to come clean but he didn't. I don't think that's sweet.'

'People do crazy things when they're in love.'

'Isn't that true,' said Cameron, darkly.

It took another half an hour to drive to the farmhouse but it felt like the longest bit of the journey to Emily.

They were so close to finding out about Dottie. This trip could mean they finally find out what happened to her, or it could lead to another dead end.

If it was a dead end, then this was it as far as Emily was concerned. She was flying to New Zealand at the end of the week and, if her Skype interview with Don and Kate went well on Monday, she would not be coming back to Britain for at least two and a half years.

★   ★   ★

A white wooden gate stood closed at the entrance to Little Coombe Farm. Emily got out to see if there was any sort of intercom system but seeing none, she opened the latch on the gate and pulled it open. Cameron drove through, she closed the gate and hopped back into the car.

The driveway was long and narrow. Fields ran along both sides but it wasn't until they turned a corner that the house came into view.

Cameron whistled and slowed the car right down so he could get a better look.

'Wow,' said Emily, 'there's some

serious money here.'

The grey stone building was on a scale with Logan Hall for size. It looked as if there had once been one very straightforward square building, a typical farmhouse in Emily's imagination, but extensions had been added to it on either side to create a long, sleek living area.

'Where do you suppose the front door is?' asked Emily.

'I'm not sure.' Cameron parked his car next to a Range Rover. 'Shall we get out and investigate?'

Dottie was unlikely to be here, Emily reminded herself. She'd be in her nineties, so even if she'd stayed working on the farm for a time after the war she wouldn't be doing so any more.

She got out and smoothed her dress down.

Cameron joined her at the front of the car.

'Ready?' he asked.

'I feel a bit intimidated,' she confessed.

'Me too.' They stood for a moment looking at the farm house. 'Still,' he said, 'we didn't come all this way just to look at a house. Let's go.'

They walked almost the whole length of the house before Emily spotted the front door. She knocked and they both stood back to wait.

A young girl, maybe ten years old with a head full of corkscrew curls, opened the door.

'Who are you?' the girl asked, looking up at them.

'Hello. I'm Emily and this is Cameron. We're looking for the owner of the farm. Is he in?'

'Mum!' called the girl, 'There's some people here to see you.'

The girl disappeared, leaving them standing in front of an open empty front door.

'This is awkward,' said Emily.

Cameron snorted. 'From the beginning this hunt has been a whole range of awkward moments. I'm getting used to them.'

A tall, broad-shouldered woman with hair as unruly as her daughter's appeared in the doorway.

'How can I help?' she asked briskly.

'Um . . . ' Emily said, not sure how to start.

'We're looking for someone,' said Cameron, 'We wondered if you could help us.'

'Tell me who you're looking for and I'll see if I can help. It'll have to be quick, though — I've loads to do.'

The woman strode out of the house and headed towards one of the outbuildings.

Emily wished she hadn't changed her comfy trainers for the sandals as she wobbled behind the woman, almost stumbling over the uneven floor of the forecourt. She felt she was going to go flying any second now.

'We're looking for someone called Dorothy Smith,' she said. 'She worked here as a Land Girl during the Second World War.'

'Why are you looking for her?'

Cameron explained as succinctly as possible, leaving out specific details of their find. 'Do you know her?' he asked when he'd finished the tale.

'Of course I know Dorothy Smith. Everyone round here does. She's a living legend.'

15

Every muscle in Cameron's back ached. He wanted to crawl into bed and let a soft mattress take his weight rather than this incredibly uncomfortable car seat. His eyes were tired from staring at the road for hours and his head was pounding from concentrating so much.

Next to him, oblivious to his discomfort, was Emily. She was clutching the piece of paper with Dottie's address on as if it were a lost scroll.

'Why can't we go this evening?' she asked.

'Because Falmouth is another hour-and-a-half's drive away and I'm exhausted. Even if I wasn't, we can hardly turn up at this time in the evening. Don't worry, we'll go first thing tomorrow morning, I promise.'

They drove in silence for a while.

Today had been a strange day. He'd

been looking forward to spending time with Emily but the drive down had been horrendous. They were both hot and grumpy and the traffic had slowed them down, making the journey far longer than it needed to be.

It hadn't helped that she'd dropped that bombshell about moving to America. He felt as if a shard of glass had lodged itself in his heart when he'd heard the news.

'Did you hear from your old boss?' he asked. He might as well find out now if she was leaving him, although she wouldn't think of it that way. This crush was obviously completely one-sided.

'Yes, I did. I've a Skype interview first thing Monday morning. Is it OK if I come in late?'

He wanted to say 'no', as the shard of glass dug deeper, but he didn't. 'Of course. Take all the time you need.'

It had been a mistake to stay with Alex, too. He'd been with her for nearly three years — they'd even lived together for a short time, but it hadn't worked out. After they'd broken up they'd promised to stay friends, and they had. They'd met many times but always in a group with other friends. They'd chatted and laughed and Cameron had prided himself on having the least messy break-up in history.

However, it was completely different in her home, where they'd spent so much time together. He knew Alex well and he could see the longing in her eyes when she looked at him. She was a lovely woman, she'd never make him feel awkward or put any pressure on him to come back to her, but if he'd known she still had feelings for him he would never have asked to stay in her house.

He knew now what unrequited love felt like — and it was painful.

The light was fading when they pulled up outside Alex's home again.

'Alex is lovely,' Emily said out of the blue.

'Yes, she is.'

He wondered if she was fishing for

information but he didn't elaborate.

Alex was as welcoming to them both as she had been when they'd arrived earlier in the day. If anything, it made Cameron feel worse.

They all headed into Alex's sleek kitchen with its stunning view through the bi-fold doors that ran along the back of the whole house. The table was laid and Alex put out lots of little dishes filled with olives, dips, breads and different types of cheeses. Cameron wondered whether the small bites would be enough to satisfy Emily's appetite, and from the dubious look on Emily's face she was wondering the same thing!

'I'll just go and freshen up. I won't be long,' said Emily and she disappeared upstairs.

Could she be going to scoff the remnants of the pizza? He grinned; it was highly possible. She had the most amazing capacity to eat.

'How did this afternoon go?' asked Alex.

'Great,' said Cameron, 'but I'll let

Emily tell you all about it. This is her adventure and she'd never forgive me if I stole her limelight.'

Alex opened the oven and took out a dish of spicy looking meatballs in a tomato sauce and some sliced potatoes.

The smell reminded Cameron of a holiday he and Alex had taken in the South of Spain. Was it a deliberate ploy to evoke memories of their happy time together? He felt mean for thinking that. Alex was a generous person, nothing more. She opened the oven again and pulled out a dish of battered squid. It looked like there would be more than enough food after all. Hopefully Emily was restraining herself upstairs.

'Are you and Emily . . . ?' Alex asked. She had her back to him but it was clear what she meant.

'No,' he answered tersely.

'Sorry, I didn't mean to pry.'

He was an idiot. He shouldn't be here. He should be in his shop. He was hurting Alex by being here and he was hurting himself by spending time with Emily when she didn't care about him in the way he wanted. What a mess!

'No, I'm sorry I . . . ' He didn't finish the sentence because Emily rejoined them.

'Hi,' she said. 'Wow! That food smells amazing. What is it all?'

Alex pointed out all the dishes and the two women were suddenly chatting about food from around the world. With their backs to Cameron they excluded him from the conversation. Instead of feeling chagrined he felt relieved that Emily had interrupted him.

What had he been about to say to Alex?

'So, Cameron tells me this afternoon went well,' said Alex, 'but he wouldn't tell me what happened. You must help yourself to whatever you want and then tell me all about it.'

They settled in their seats and Cameron pulled up a chair to join them. Emily started to help herself, putting a little taste of something from every dish onto her plate.

'It turns out,' she said, after she'd told Alex all about the house and meeting the farmer, 'that Dorothy Smith stayed on at the farm after the war. She built it up into this huge success and lots of her products are in the major supermarkets. You should have seen the farmhouse, Alex — it was massive — she must have made a fortune!

'Apparently, she was this really formidable figure who ran the farm until she was in her eighties. She only retired five years ago, but — and I think this is the best bit of the story — when she retired she moved in with her daughter.'

'Why's that the best bit?' Alex asked.

'Because,' she said, waving her fork about, 'Her daughter must be Harry Logan's.'

Alex met Cameron's eyes. She obviously agreed with him that this was a big leap. Emily caught the look.

'I know Cameron thinks I'm crazy

but she obviously didn't marry again because she's still Dorothy Smith. So I think she became pregnant with Harry Logan's child right before he went off to war. If she stayed at the farm she could pretend that she'd married before she became pregnant. If she went home to Lentworth everyone would know that wasn't true. So she stayed.'

'Didn't the other Dorothy Smith say she was incredibly thin at Harry's funeral?' Cameron pointed out.

'Perhaps she was one of these women who are very sick in the first twelve weeks. Or maybe Dorothy doesn't remember it correctly. It was seventy years ago, after all.'

'It's possible,' said Alex, politely.

Cameron took a sip of wine and watched as the two of them discussed Dottie's reaction to finding out she was pregnant and that the baby's father had died.

He wasn't convinced this was what had happened. Emily had wanted to believe that Dottie had been faithful to

Harry Logan's memory right from the beginning of the treasure hunt. It was why she was so desperate to return the locket. But she was putting her own feelings onto Dottie. Perhaps the belief that someone else had stayed true to their first love after death legitimised her own decision to stay single.

There were many other possibilities . . . maybe Dottie had married but kept her own name. Perhaps she'd adopted a child. He'd said as much in the car on the drive from the farmhouse but Emily didn't want to hear it. She'd made her mind up. Cameron hoped that whatever the truth was, she wouldn't end up getting hurt. Not when she'd made so much effort to return the locket.

As the meal wore on Emily became much quieter and Cameron was forced to keep the conversation going. He searched for uncontroversial subjects but even he was bored by his ten-minute monologue on surfing!

It didn't help that she kept flicking glances between him and Alex — and when she wasn't doing that, Alex kept flicking glances between him and Emily. They both wanted to know if there was something between him and the other woman.

He was close to blurting out the truth when Emily started clearing away the dishes.

'There's no need for you to do that,' said Alex, resting a hand on Emily's arm. 'You must be exhausted after the day you've had. I'll clear up if you'd like to go and sit in the lounge.'

'Well, if you really don't mind I think I'll head up to bed. I'm shattered.'

'Of course not, you go on up.'

Emily said her goodnights and then she hot-footed it upstairs, leaving Cameron alone with Alex. He supposed he wouldn't get away with saying he was tired and disappearing upstairs too, so he gathered up the dishes and took them through to the kitchen. Alex joined him at the kitchen sink and for a while they washed and dried in silence.

'Emily seems like a really nice girl,'

said Alex after a while.

'She is,' Cameron replied. 'I owe her a massive favour. She's done loads of work for me and I've paid her virtually nothing.'

'Hence the trip down here.'

'Exactly.'

Of course that wasn't the only reason. There was also his hopeless crush on her.

'I spoke to your dad the other day.' Alex changed the subject. 'He told me he was thinking of taking up speed-dating.'

'He's trying to rope me into that.'

'Are you going to?'

'Never in a million years.'

Alex laughed. She and Alistair had got on well and had kept in touch even after she and Cameron had split up. Alistair had never understood why Cameron had ended things with her.

'Are you seeing anyone?' Alex asked.

'Not at the moment.'

There was a pause in the conversation when he guessed he was supposed to ask her the same question. He didn't. It was best not to open that can of worms.

'Me neither,' said Alex, telling him anyway.

They finished tidying the rest of the kitchen in silence. Cameron remembered where everything went from when he'd stayed before and it was easy to slip into their old routine.

He loved this house. It was a bit like the Tardis; nothing to look at from the front but once you stepped inside it was light and airy and the uninterrupted views of the sea were magnificent. He'd understood why Alex had wanted to live here when she'd inherited the property. The house had needed updating and her job was freelance so she didn't need to live in London, where they'd lived together in a pokey little flat.

She'd moved with the intention of commuting back and forth to see Cameron and her freelance contacts while she made the house into luxury accommodation. He'd been happy to travel down to see her every other weekend and they'd carried on like that for almost a year. He'd have happily carried on indefinitely but Alex decided she wanted to stay in Paignton permanently. She'd asked him to move in with her but he'd realised that he didn't want to.

He was already deep in discussions with Paul about setting up McKenzie & Brown's and he wanted to do that more than move to Paignton where he couldn't see a future for himself. If a fabulous house and a gorgeous woman weren't enough to entice him to move, he'd reasoned, then the relationship wasn't working.

Had he been wrong? Was his decision not to carry on with the relationship based more on the fear of becoming his parents than anything to do with Alex?

'Would you like another drink?' Alex asked once everything was put away.

'Thanks, but I think I'd better head up too. Today was exhausting and I've got even more driving to do tomorrow.'

She came and stood in front of him.

'Cam . . . ' she said softly.

He looked into her large brown eyes. It would be so easy to kiss her, to take up where they left off. Her expression told him she would welcome him back.

Maybe his father was right and it was time for him to settle down. A future with Emily was a pipe dream, but with Alex . . .

He leaned towards her.

16

Emily didn't know what to make of Cameron's mood this morning. He was quiet and distracted. Every time she attempted conversation, he managed to grunt a two-syllable response before lapsing back into silence.

Was it something to do with Alex? Had something happened after Emily had gone to bed? She'd noticed Alex was still in love with Cameron but she didn't think he was aware of it. Some people were so blind when it came to love.

Cameron deserved someone special in his life and Alex seemed to be a beautiful and intelligent woman; he'd be lucky to have her.

The thought of them together made her stomach feel tight and uncomfortable but she didn't know why. It wasn't as if she wanted him for herself, was it?

Perhaps he was just sore from all the driving he'd done. She hadn't really fancied getting in the car this morning either.

'Are you OK?' she asked.

'Yep,' he said, 'great.'

Silence again. It was going to be a long day.

★ ★ ★

Emily's stomach clenched as they passed the sign welcoming them to Falmouth. Very soon they would meet Dottie and reunite her with her necklace. Suddenly she didn't want this all to end. It had been fun hunting for Dottie — and once it was all over she had to get on with the next chapter of her life.

'Shall we stop for a coffee?' said Emily

Cameron glanced across at her. 'I thought you were eager to get to Dottie.'

'I am, it's just . . . '

He reached over and his long fingers

curled around her hand.

'Are you worried about meeting Dottie after all this time? I'll stop if you really want to, but it's only going to put off the inevitable.'

She sighed. 'You're right. Let's carry on.'

He squeezed her hand and went to let go but she tightened her grip. They held hands for a few minutes, Emily taking comfort from the warmth of his hand. The muscles in her neck slowly relaxed and her stomach felt settled again.

Everything would be fine.

He cleared his throat. 'I have to change gear.'

'Sorry.' She let go of his hand, resisting the urge to take it back again once he'd completed the gear change.

'No problem,' he said and grinned. Whatever mood had been affecting him had disappeared and he was back to his normal self. 'We're only a few minutes away now,' he said. 'Do you know what you're going to say?'

'Sort of, although I'm more concerned about her reaction. What if she just says, 'Great, thanks,' takes the necklace and shuts the door in our faces?'

He turned the car towards Swanpool, the final leg of their journey.

'Well, we'll have returned the necklace, which I thought was the point of the whole exercise.'

Emily laughed. 'It is, but I want to find out her side of the story. I feel she owes me.'

'We'll hold the necklace to ransom, then. To get it back she has to tell all.'

Emily laughed again. 'Good idea!' she said.

They travelled along the coast for a short while and then took a turning to the left. There were hardly any houses on this stretch of the coast and most of them were hidden from the road by large leafy gardens.

'This trip is making me feel very poor,' said Cameron. 'I own a pokey flat in Brighton that would fit into some of the garages we've passed. And I'm even too broke to live in that.'

'I don't even own a flat,' said Emily.

'It's not too late to turn round. We could always flog the necklace. It's worth a fair bit.'

Emily snorted with laughter. 'Why didn't you say that when we found it? We could be in the Bahamas by now!'

He grinned and stopped the car. 'This is it.'

Emily looked at the large detached bungalow with its wide open driveway.

'Ready?' he asked.

She checked for the tenth time that the locket and letter were still in her handbag. They were.

'Yes,' she said and clambered out of the car.

They walked slowly up the driveway side by side. At the entrance Emily took a deep breath and rang the doorbell.

A short, slender woman, possibly in her seventies, with gunmetal grey hair and a mischievous smile answered.

'Ah,' she said. 'You've arrived. Do come in.'

The welcome was so unexpected that neither of them moved to follow the woman.

'Mum's really keen to know what you've found of hers. Come along in,' the lady called out.

Cameron nudged Emily in the back.

'The farmer must have phoned ahead. Come on, let's go.'

The hallway alone was larger than Emily's bedroom at her parents' house. Cameron gave a low whistle of appreciation.

The lady's head popped out of one of the doorways to the left of the hallway.

'I'm Alice, by the way. Come on through. Mum's in the sunroom. No need to worry about your shoes.'

She disappeared again.

'This whole experience is getting weirder by the second,' whispered Cameron.

Emily nudged him in the ribs. He laughed and she stepped close to him as they went through the doorway and made their way to the back of the house.

The sunroom was a large conservatory with amazing views of Swanpool beach but Emily only had eyes for the tiny woman who sat in a large cushioned armchair. She was beaming at them from behind a pair of tortoiseshell glasses. Her grey hair was worn in a stylish bob and she wore expensive clothes on her thin frame.

'Come in, come in,' said the tiny lady, who could only be Dottie. 'I'm so glad you're here. When Sandra rang last night to say two people were looking for me she didn't mention how gorgeous you both were. Look at you!' she said to Cameron. 'You're beautiful! A girl could drown in your eyes! If only I was seventy years younger!' She let out a peal of laughter.

'Mum, leave the poor boy alone,' said Alice. 'You're embarrassing him.'

Cameron didn't look embarrassed to Emily — if anything he looked incredibly pleased with himself, but then she already knew that he was an incorrigible flirt.

'And you,' said Dottie, nodding to Emily. 'Come and sit by me, my dear, and tell me what you've found. Ever since Sandra rang I've been trying to work it out and then it suddenly dawned on me in the early hours of this morning. Is it my locket?'

Dottie patted the chair nearest to her and Emily went to sit next to her.

This meeting wasn't going at all how she'd envisaged. All the words she'd planned dried up.

'Em . . . yes, the locket . . . ' was all she could think of to say.

Cameron sat next to her as she pulled the necklace and the letter out of her handbag and held them out to Dottie.

The old woman's hands were spotted brown with age but her grip was firm as she took the items from Emily and slowly took the letter out of the envelope.

She read it and then passed it to her daughter. Then she gently took the locket out of its protective case and, for the first time in seventy years, opened the clasp to look at Harry.

'Ah . . . ' she said, 'Poor, sweet Harry. Here, Alice, take a look.'

She handed the locket to her daughter.

'Who's Harry, Mum?'

'He was my fiancé before the war. He was such a handsome lad and so gentle. He was shot dead very early on in the war. Poor chap.'

'Your fiancé? Did Dad know about this?'

Alice wasn't the only one reeling!

'Poor chap' and 'Dad' were just a few of the words that had thrown this whole tale on its head! Clearly, Emily had been wrong about a lot of things.

She clasped her hands tightly together. Cameron reached over and covered them with one of his. It was the most natural thing in the world to unclasp her hands and entwine her fingers with his. She didn't look at him.

'Of course your dad knew about Harry. Why don't you make us all a cup of tea, darling, and I'll tell everyone the whole story.'

She turned to look at Cameron and Emily. 'While Alice is making us the tea will you tell me how you came across the locket? I searched and searched for it at the time and I couldn't find it anywhere.'

So Emily told her all about finding the locket in a secret compartment and how the search for Dottie had led them to Dorothy Smith in Appleby and Paul Standen in Lentworth. She told her about Paul Standen's role in the disappearance of the locket.

By the time she'd finished they all needed another cup of tea.

'You already know a lot of the story, then,' said Dottie, taking a sip of her fresh cup. 'I'm amazed at Paul, hiding the necklace. He was such a gentle soul, always concerned more about his flowers than anything else. I was mad for him, but once I spent a bit more time with him that faded. He needed a gentle wife to match his personality and that person was never going to be me.

'I was already keen to get away from him by the time I met Harry. That sounds awful, doesn't it? But, it's the truth. I can still remember the first time I set eyes on Harry. He was so tall and strong — a bit like you,' she said, turning to Cameron.

Emily smirked as a hint of red stole up Cameron's neck.

'But whereas you're dark, Harry was blond with striking blue eyes. Like a classical Grecian God.'

'Mum, don't exaggerate. She always does, you know — you have to watch her. Now is this going to be a long story, Mum? If so I'll go and get some cake.'

'When does anyone ever need an excuse for cake? Do get some, dear.'

Alice disappeared into the kitchen, taking the now empty teapot with her.

'I never exaggerate, don't listen to her.'

'Yes, you do!' Alice shouted from the kitchen.

Dottie laughed and winked at them both.

Emily felt strangely disconnected from proceedings. She'd expected to find a woman dignified in both age and grief and instead she'd found a loud, gregarious lady who was flirting with a man sixty years younger than her!

'Now where was I? Oh yes, meeting Harry Logan . . . Now everyone in the village told me to stay away from him. There were all sorts of horror stories of young girls going to work in these big houses and being cast off when they got pregnant by one of the owners. I was determined that wasn't going to happen to me no matter how handsome Harry was.'

Was she about to tell them it *had* happened to her? Had Dottie married someone else to protect her child with Harry?

'But Harry was very persistent. He was wearing me down and he finally won me over when he took me rowing on the lake at Logan Hall. It was a beautiful summer's afternoon. Harry rowed out quite far and then we both leaned back in the boat and let it just drift.

'Ah, I can still remember the sound of the water lapping against the side of the boat and feel the warmth of the sun on my face.

'We talked and talked and I realised that he was a good man, full of determination to change the world around him for the better. That afternoon in the summer sun was magical. A slice of idyll when the rest of Europe was fermenting with badness.

'We were so naïve, so full of big ideas. I was mad for him after that. His parents were a little upset when he told them he was going to marry me. I think they had plans for him to marry some girl from his own class, but he was such a charmer was Harry that he soon brought them round.

'But then there was the war, and then he was gone. Just like that. Such a waste of a good human being. But then so many boys of our generation were lost. War is a terrible thing.'

Alice brought out slices of home-made Victoria sponge and passed them round. Emily didn't really feel like eating but she took a bite out of politeness — and then another one because it was so good and she never could pass up a delicious cake, not even when she was as shaken as this.

She kept one hand entangled with Cameron's. He was her anchor.

'What happened when you moved to Little Coombe Farm?' he asked.

'That was a big shock,' Dottie answered. 'I thought I knew what hard work was but I had no idea! We were up at dawn and working until there was no light left. I hated it at first.'

'Did you?' Alice asked, looking incredulous.

'Oh yes, I thought it was awful. I couldn't wait to get back to Harry and become lady of the manor. I wanted to crack on with our big ideas for social reform — but obviously without getting my hands dirty.' Dottie laughed. 'I was a bit hoity-toity, I'm afraid. But then Harry died and the hard work became a solace. A year on after Harry died and I realised that I not only enjoyed the work but I was good at it, too. And now we get to the good bit.'

Dottie stopped and winked at Emily and Cameron. Emily swallowed several times; she couldn't imagine what was coming next.

'I met Freddie, the son of the owners of Little Coombe Farm. He came back on leave. I didn't even notice him at first. He was quiet, steady . . . the exact opposite of me.

'We didn't get on all that well to start with either. It was his home, but his father had been very ill so I'd taken on some of the running. He didn't like the new way I was doing things. Then his father died and he had no choice but to leave the farm to my management.

'The next time he was granted leave he saw that I was making a difference. The leave after that he asked me if he could court me and I thought, why not? He wasn't my type but men were scarce on the ground, you see. I didn't expect to fall in love with him. I certainly didn't expect to marry him and have five daughters, either, but that's what happened.

'I'm sorry that Harry died. I wish he hadn't but I don't regret the fabulous life I had with my Fred. He died eight years ago and there's not a day that goes by when I don't think about him.'

Emily looked at Alice, and saw there were tears in her eyes, but she was smiling at her mother.

'Having said all that, I wouldn't say no if *you* wanted to whisk me off for a whirlwind fling, young man!' Dottie winked at Cameron and Emily was amazed to see a blush creep up his neck and flush his face.

Dottie spotted it and her hearty laugh pealed out again.

'I'm only joking with you. I know I can't compete with your beautiful girlfriend here.'

Dottie gestured to Emily, who felt a blush of her own spreading across her cheeks. Whether it was being called beautiful or Cameron's girlfriend, she wasn't sure.

'Let's have some more cake,' said Dottie. 'And then you can tell me all about yourselves.'

'Mum, they might not have time.'

'We have plenty of time,' said Cameron.

He did most of the talking, probably recognising that Emily wasn't keen to talk about her past, and she was grateful.

She wasn't sure how she felt about this morning's revelations. Was Dottie atypical in finding love again — or was it Emily's vow to remain single that was unusual?

She wanted a bit of quietness to process what they'd found out — quietness she was unlikely to find near the formidable Dottie.

17

Emily's head was back against the head rest and her eyes were closed, but Cameron doubted she was asleep.

She'd been so quiet since they'd left Dottie's house. Any attempt he'd made to talk about what had happened there had been deflected with talk about the weather or the traffic — and now this fake sleep.

What was it that had bothered Emily the most? Dottie's remarriage, or her regret that she'd lost touch with her dearest friend after Harry's death because anything to do with Lentworth had been too painful?

Emily never talked about friends. She didn't go and visit any and he'd never found her texting anyone. She must have had friends before Johnny's death, but where had they all gone now? Cameron hadn't thought about it before, but now it was really bothering him. Had she really cut herself off from everyone? If so, was this round the world trip really about moving forward or was it more running away?

Dottie's excitement at having Dorothy's telephone number had been far greater than receiving her locket. She'd told them she would phone Dorothy straight away so as not to waste any more time. Cameron hoped that, at their ages, they would have time to get to know one another again.

'Emily?' he whispered.

She opened her eyes and turned to look at him. Not asleep then.

'We're nearly home. Do you want to stop and get some food before we get back?' he offered.

'Do you mind if we don't?' she said. 'I'm so tired. I just want to go to bed. You must be exhausted too. Thanks so much for organising this weekend and for driving all that way.'

'It was no problem.'

That wasn't totally true. It had been

hard work and stressful at times, but he'd spent the time with Emily, which had made it worthwhile.

After they'd pulled up and he'd finally, blessedly, turned off the engine, she gave him a quick hug and a kiss on the cheek before walking up the driveway to her parents' house. Before she let herself in, she turned and gave him a small smile and then she was gone.

In less than a week she wouldn't be living there any more. His heart lurched painfully. Should he tell her how he felt, or let her go?

★   ★   ★

Alistair was in the kitchen chatting on the phone when he got in. He saluted Cameron with his bottle of beer and started to wind down the conversation. Cameron helped himself to a beer from the fridge and then pulled up a chair to the breakfast bar.

'How did it go?' asked Alistair. No

reply. 'That bad, eh?'

'I should never have stayed at Alex's house.'

'I thought that was a strange thing to do when the girl's still in love with you.'

'Why didn't you tell me?'

'I thought you knew. It was so obvious. Did she bring it up? Did you . . . you know?'

'No.'

He wasn't going to tell his father that he'd been sorely tempted to rekindle things with Alex but had stopped himself just in time. It wasn't fair on Alex. He'd only have been using her to help him cope with Emily's lack of interest and he'd have hated himself afterwards. Alex was lovely . . . but he didn't love her.

'How about Emily — any progress there?'

'No, there's the opposite of progress. She's got a job interview on Monday.'

'She was hardly likely to stay as your underpaid assistant forever. The girl's got talent.'

'The job's in America.'

'Ah . . .'

They sipped their beers in silence for a moment.

'You could tell her how you feel about her.'

Cameron snorted and shook his head.

'I think I'll go take a shower.'

'Oh — Maddie called over yesterday and said she's going to have a leaving do for Emily on Thursday evening asked did we want to come. I said we would.'

Cameron stopped in his tracks.

'I hope she's not planning a repeat of that party — that was torture for Emily.'

'It's going to be just us and them.' Alistair paused. 'Maddie's convinced there's a romance between the two of you, you know. I think she's hoping you're going to stop Emily from going.'

'That's not going to happen. She doesn't think of me in that way. As far as she's concerned we're just good friends.'

'Maybe Maddie knows more than you think. Perhaps it's not as hopeless as you suppose.'

Sometimes Cameron thought that too.

Whether Emily was aware of it or not, she stepped closer to him when she was worried about something, as if his presence gave her the reassurance she needed. When he put on certain clothes her eyes would shine with approval and she got slightly shirty if she thought he was overly flirting with any of the customers — which he'd found himself doing sometimes, just to get a reaction.

Still, it wasn't enough. She might value their friendship, might even find him attractive — but she was still going to leave to work in America and there was nothing he could do to stop her.

At least the leaving party would give him the opportunity to give Emily her leaving present — not that she'd have much use for it now. He half hoped she wouldn't get the job, even though it was what she wanted.

★ ★ ★

Monday morning came with the news that Emily had been successful and the job was hers if she wanted it.

Cameron did a reasonable job of pretending to be happy for her but he left the shop at lunchtime and went for a run. He pushed himself as far as he could until his burning lungs hurt almost as much as his heart.

Before he knew it, it was Thursday, the day before the only girl he'd ever loved was due to fly out of his life, never to return.

18

Maddie was fretting. 'Have you packed sun cream, Emily?' she asked. 'You're so fair, you must take extra special care of your skin. I've some factor fifty downstairs . . . '

'Yes Mum, I've packed sun cream.' Emily didn't point out that she was well aware of her own skin tone. 'Spring will only just be starting in New Zealand when I arrive. It'll be fairly mild.'

She might as well have not spoken because her mother was in full fussing mode. Emily half-expected her to unpack the already completed backpack to check she'd remembered to put in her underwear!

'It doesn't seem like very much stuff, Emily. You're going away for such a long time and you're taking less than I would on a weekend away.'

'That's because you always overpack, Mum.'

'That's not true! I always take exactly the right amount.' She opened Emily's wardrobe and pulled out a pale-blue hoodie. 'You should take this; it's versatile.'

Emily took the hoodie out of her hands and put it back in the wardrobe.

'They do have shops in New Zealand, Mum. If I'm in desperately need of something I can buy it. Stop panicking.'

'I can see that I'm not needed.' Maddie flounced. 'I'll go and check on the food. You stay up here and get some rest. It'll be a long day tomorrow.'

She dashed out of the room and Emily smiled. Maddie didn't really want her to rest — she wanted her out of the way. There was lots of unusual movement going on downstairs and she'd heard some muffled swear words. She was cooking up some sort of surprise and Emily would spoil it if she went downstairs.

She knew it wasn't a surprise party because she had made her mother promise she wouldn't do that to her. They'd had words over the last soirée and the horde of eligible bachelors thrown her way. Emily had made her swear she wouldn't try and set her up with anyone ever again.

So whatever the surprise was, it was likely to be a pleasant one. She hoped.

Emily flipped open her laptop and checked her emails. She'd finally told her friends she wasn't going to make the university reunion. Instead of leaving it at that, as she'd planned to originally, she'd asked two of the girls she'd been closest to if they'd like to meet up with her somewhere on her travels. She wasn't convinced it was going to happen but there were tentative talks about them meeting up in Thailand for two weeks.

Even if it didn't happen, she wasn't going to neglect her old friendships any more. That much she'd learned from her meeting with Dottie.

She had an email from one of the girls, suggesting possible flights. Perhaps the meeting would happen after all. She typed out a quick reply and then closed her laptop down.

Moving her large rucksack off her

bed, she set it down on the floor by the door, then checked her handbag for her passport, tickets, money and phone. They were all there — as they had been the last ten times she'd checked. She set that down by the door, too.

She was ready to go.

Going over to the window she had a last look at her favourite view. After a while of watching the water she looked down into Alistair's garden. Neither he nor Cameron were out there, but that was hardly surprising. Maddie had invited them over for dinner so they were probably getting ready. Hopefully Cameron would be wearing his green shirt this evening; he looked good in it.

Emily flopped onto her bed. She shouldn't be thinking of him in those terms but over the last few days that sort of unwanted thought kept popping into her head.

They'd sat together while she'd tried, and failed, to explain how to run the website and the whole time she'd been aware of how close their arms were. She could hear him breathing and smell the citrus scent of his shower gel. As her fingers brushed over the keys she'd wanted him to take her hands in his again, to feel the warmth of his fingers as they curled around hers.

It hadn't happened and afterwards, when she was safely away from him, she was glad because she didn't want those kinds of feelings awakened.

She glanced at her clock. Cameron and Alistair should be here by now. Had enough time passed for her to go downstairs? The muffled sounds had stopped a few minutes ago. It was probably safe to go down and see everyone.

She took a deep breath. She mustn't be emotional tonight. It was time for celebration, not for sadness.

Emily jumped up and checked herself in the mirror. Lying on the pillow had mussed her hair, so she ran a comb through to try and tame it but it resulted in making it frizz badly so she used some pins to put it back in a simple up-do. It wasn't brilliant but it would have to do.

She grimaced at her pale skin. The summer had been gorgeous so why was she still just a shade off-white in colour? She brushed a little bronzer over her cheeks which made her skin look a little healthier. She dropped the brush back in her make-up bag and she spotted her lipstick. She made a snap decision to wear some tonight. It was her leaving party, after all, so she might as well dress up a little.

She took a step back and looked in the full-length mirror. She was wearing jeans and a pink surf T-shirt — definitely not dressy enough. Her wardrobe was devoid of her favourite clothes but there was no way she was unpacking her backpack to find something suitable. It would give Maddie the opening to fill the backpack with unwanted clothes and then she'd need a crane to lift it!

There was always the indecently short black dress, the one she'd rejected last week for being far too young for her. Without pausing too much to think about it she tugged off her clothes and pulled the dress over her head. It wasn't as short as she remembered and came down to mid-thigh, which was just about acceptable. The neckline was a bit low. She pulled up the front while also tugging down on the hem. When she was satisfied that enough of her flesh was covered she decided she looked ready for a party now.

'Emily,' Maddie called up, 'are you coming down, love?'

'I'm on my way,' she called back.

She ran down the two flights of stairs and stopped at the door to the lounge. A *Good Luck* banner had been pinned to the lounge door. She touched the silvery paper and it crinkled softly under her fingertips.

Maddie opened the door a crack.

'Are you coming in?' she asked.

'Of course,' said Emily, her voice thick.

Maddie opened the door wider and Emily stepped in to the lounge. The first person she saw was Cameron — who was wearing her favourite green shirt and smiling at her from across the room. For a moment all she could see was him, then she spotted what he was leaning on.

'What's that doing here?' she exclaimed.

'It's your leaving present,' Cameron said. 'I know you said you can't take it on the plane to New Zealand with you, but it's here for you when you get back.'

Cameron stood up to his full height so Emily could get close to her present.

'I can't accept this,' she said, running her hands lovingly over the antique writing desk. 'You can't spare it. Anyway, I thought you'd sold it?'

'I did — to you,' he said, grinning. 'Emily, I could never repay you for everything you've done for me. Please. It's yours.'

'I love it, Cameron.'

He laughed. 'I know you do.'

The conversation carried on around her as she explored her desk. She pulled open the letter drawers and imagined what she would put in each one. The writing area was big enough for her laptop. She'd have to ask Cameron to make her a chair to match. It would need to be exactly the right height so she didn't get a crick in her neck while typing. She would pay him for that, although it wouldn't equal the generosity of this gift.

She turned to thank him again and saw that he was watching her, smiling softly. She smiled back at him.

Maddie had made all Emily's favourites for dinner — slow roast lamb with heaps of vegetables and crispy roast potatoes. Emily piled her plate high; she didn't know when she would next get to eat Maddie's cooking. Dessert was home-made lemon meringue pie. Ever since she'd been a child this was her favourite. Shop bought ones didn't come close to the crumbly pastry base with the light, lemon-flavoured middle and the melt-in-the-mouth gooey topping.

Emily was glad she'd worn the dress because her jeans would have popped open after she asked for a second helping!

'Thanks, Mum. That was amazing,' she said when she finally put her spoon down.

'It was a triumph, Maddie,' agreed Alistair. 'You're such a fabulous cook. I'm much better looking than Tom, why don't you come and live with me instead?'

Everyone laughed.

'I hear you've been on a date with the same woman more than once,' said Maddie archly. 'What's going on there?'

Alistair shifted on his seat a little.

'Yes, well, um . . . I do seem to have met someone . . . ' His ears turned pink.

'You can tell us all about it while we clean up,' said Maddie. 'Tom, Alistair, let's clear up and give these young ones time to talk.'

Maddie grabbed the dishes and Tom and Alistair dutifully took the remaining platters.

'Your Dad's got a girlfriend?' Emily asked, the wine making her feel emotional. 'How cute!'

'Let's not get too carried away. I think they've only been on four dates so far.'

'But he never normally makes it past the second one, so this is lovely news.'

Cameron leaned forward so his elbows were on the table. Emily mirrored his movements until they were nearly touching.

'He met her on the day of the launch. She was one of the first people through the door and she's been in quite a lot since. I thought it was the stock she was interested in but it turns out not to be the case. She's still bought quite a bit while she's been waiting for Dad to ask her out.'

They both giggled.

Cameron dropped his right arm down to pick up his wine glass. His long fingers curled around the stem as he lifted it to his mouth.

Emily watched the movement intently.

'You have lovely hands,' she blurted out.

Cameron's wine glass stopped at his lips. He looked at her over the edge of his glass.

'Thanks. So do you.'

279

Emily glanced down at her own hands. They were so pale and small in comparison to his. She reached over and took his free hand in her own. As always it was warm. She brought it closer and saw numerous little scars running across the back of it — from his carpentry probably. She turned it over and traced the creases with her fingertip. Next to her Cameron was very still.

'Emily,' he whispered. 'How much have you had to drink?'

Emily looked at her empty wine glass. 'Quite a bit,' she said.

He laughed and laced his fingers through hers. She didn't pull her fingers away and for a while they sat there holding hands in contented silence.

The room spun slowly when she eventually got up. Enough for her to think that tomorrow might be quite hard work.

She forgot about trying to look sober when she went to say goodbye to Alistair. She threw her arms around his bulk and mumbled words about how lovely it had been to live next door to him for a while and how she hoped his new girlfriend would prove to be someone very special.

Alistair chuckled. 'The pleasure's been all mine. I hope you have a glorious journey around the world, and we'll see you when you get back.'

He kissed the top of her head and then headed out of the front door.

Then it was just Cameron and her in the hallway.

'I'll pick you up at seven tomorrow,' he said. 'Do I get a hug as well?'

She flung her arms around him and buried her face in his chest. She inhaled his unique citrus smell as he held her tightly.

'I'm going to miss you, Emily Robson.'

She looked up at him. 'I'll miss you too.'

Like on the night of Maddie's party he tightened his arms and leaned down to brush her lips with his. Then he let go, smiled sadly at her and left.

Despite the amount she'd had to drink Emily found it difficult to sleep.

She was attracted to Cameron, she had to admit that to herself now. No matter how hard she'd tried to suppress her feelings she also had to confess that she liked him a lot — and not just as a friend. Feelings she'd thought were impossible were whizzing around in her.

In the early hours of the morning she pulled back the covers and opened her curtains. Everything was quiet and still. She could make out the red light on top of the observation tower but the sea was nothing but inky blackness.

After a few minutes she flopped back on her bed and flipped on her bedside light. She picked up the picture of Johnny she always kept close.

'What do you think?' she whispered.

His picture smiled back at her but didn't answer.

'I know you'd like him,' she said. 'He's funny, smart and kind. But is he worth the risk of having all those feelings again?' Then she laughed. 'I'm assuming he feels something for me, which is a little bit arrogant, don't you think?

'This is last night nerves, isn't it? I'm worried about going to the other side of the world on my own and so I'm looking for reasons to pull out. Then there was all that wine . . . and the flickering candlelight . . . and sitting by a handsome man. Anyone would have felt the stirrings of romance.'

She put Johnny's picture back. The trip was the right thing to do and she wasn't going to back out because she'd got a little tipsy and turned all gooey-eyed over Cameron. She was just like all the other women who looked at him and turned to jelly. She'd feel differently in the morning.

Finally, she managed to fall asleep.

★　★　★

It seemed like she'd barely closed her eyes before the alarm was ringing. She pulled herself out of bed, quickly showered and dressed. There was nothing else to be done other than eat breakfast and leave.

She was ready.

Both her parents were already downstairs. Tom was dressed but Maddie was still wearing her neck-to-floor dressing gown while she prepared a small mountain of food.

'What's all this for?' Emily asked, gesturing to the tower of sandwiches, cereal bars and fruit.

'Well, it's for you, of course. You've no idea when your next meal will be, have you?'

'I'm pretty certain I'll have at least three meals on the plane.'

'But what if it's delayed?'

'The airport has these things called restaurants where you can buy food. A novel concept but . . . '

'It'll cost you a fortune to buy a meal from one of those places,' her mother said, ignoring the sarcasm as she began piling the food into a carrier bag.

Emily stopped her adding three bottles of water. 'I can't take that through security, Mum.'

Maddie took two out but left one.

'For the journey to the airport,' she said.

The doorbell rang before Emily could point out that it was only slightly over half an hour's journey. She went to open the front door. Cameron was standing on the doorstep in his usual jeans and T-shirt combination.

Emily's heartbeat picked up a gear. *He's a friend, that's all*, she reminded herself.

'Hey,' he said. 'All set?'

Cameron took her bags out to the car while she went to tell her parents she was leaving now.

Maddie pulled Emily to her for a fierce hug. Emily relaxed into her tight grip and let the comforting smell of magnolia wash over her.

'You'll Skype us as soon as you get there.'

'Yes, Mum.'

'You'll stay safe and not go anywhere dodgy.'

'Yes, Mum.'

'We'll come over and visit as soon as you're settled in America.'

'I'll look forward to it.'

Maddie let go and Emily turned to her dad. Tom wasn't great when it came to expressing emotion but Emily could tell how he felt by his expression.

'Oh, Dad,' she said and wrapped her arms around his solid frame. 'I'm not going forever.'

He hugged her and patted her awkwardly on the back. 'I know, love.'

Maddie and Tom stood on their doorstep, watching as Emily climbed into Cameron's car. Tom's arm was wrapped tightly around his wife's shoulder. They stood there waving as Cameron drove slowly down the road. Emily saw that they were still waving as the car turned a corner and she lost sight of them.

She puffed out her cheeks and let out a long breath of air.

'That was harder than I thought it

would be,' she said.

Cameron smiled. 'Saying goodbye is never easy. Especially when they're your parents and they love you so much.'

'Yes. That's not made me feel any better.'

Cameron smiled. 'Don't worry about it. I'm sure they're over you already. In fact, Maddie is probably planning a party to celebrate having the place to themselves again!'

Emily bashed him lightly on the arm. 'You're so mean!'

He grinned and she watched as he changed gear. Had his muscles always looked that defined? How come she'd been with him for three months and not really noticed before?

'Have I got some breakfast on my face?' he asked lightly.

Emily jumped, she hadn't realised she'd been staring and blushed at having been caught.

For the rest of the journey she kept her eyes on the road and talked about the places she was planning to visit.

As they got closer to the airport her conversation dried up and for the last two miles they sat in silence. She didn't know what he was thinking but she was desperately trying not to cry.

Cameron parked up the car and said calmly, 'I'll see you to check in.'

He pulled her backpack out of the car and swung it onto his back. He'd hefted it up, expecting it to be heavy, and it slapped hard onto his back because it wasn't. He laughed.

'You're not taking much, are you?' he commented.

'Don't you start. Mum's been on at me to pack the entire contents of my wardrobe. If I've forgotten anything I'll buy it out there.'

'It was a compliment,' he said. 'I can never decide what I need, so I end up taking everything I own with me. When I get where I'm going I realise I only needed enough stuff to fill a carrier bag.'

Emily smiled and Cameron held out a hand. It felt like the most natural thing in the world to take it and hold on to it tightly as they walked towards check in.

'Here we are,' he said unnecessarily when they reached the large queue of travellers all wheeling giant suitcases.

Emily counted three rows snaking backwards. Even though it seemed to be moving quickly, she would have to join them soon if she wanted a stress-free progress through security.

'Thanks for everything, Cameron. I've had a great summer. It was kind of you to follow me on the mad quest to find Dottie when you should have told me to get lost.'

'It was fun,' he said. 'It's not often you get to trek across the country and meet crazy nonagenarians.'

She looked up at him. He was smiling but his eyes were sad. They were still holding hands.

'Look, Emily . . . '

He faltered, looked around himself before going on, 'I know you're going off to a well-paid job where they're going to use your talents and where you're bound to become their star, but if you change your mind and want your under-valued, underpaid and overworked job at Home to Home back, it will always be open for you.'

'Thanks,' Emily said softly.

They stood gazing at each other for a moment before Emily rose up onto her tiptoes and gently kissed him.

The kiss started off soft but when Cameron laced his fingers through her hair she pulled him closer. It was all the signal he needed to deepen the kiss. Moments passed and all she could think of was the feel of his lips against hers and the strength of his arms as he held her close.

He lifted his head and looked at her sadly.

'I guess this is it,' he said, his voice unsteady.

He didn't let her go.

She nodded and wrapped her arms around his waist and held on tightly breathing him in for the last time. Her tears would be held back no longer and one leaked, rolling slowly down her cheek.

She took a deep breath, wiped the tears away with the back of her hand and stepped away from him. She picked up her backpack.

'Come back to me, Emily,' he said, so softly she wouldn't have heard it if they hadn't been standing so close.

She looked up into his eyes and saw that they were shining with unshed tears.

She stood on tiptoes to kiss his cheek.

'Bye, Cameron,' she said softly.

Then she walked away from him.

19

Cameron nearly hurled his phone across the room in sheer frustration. 'Why won't this work?' he growled.

Alistair popped his head round the storeroom door. 'What's wrong?' he asked.

'I'm trying to email this photograph to Emily but I can't get it to attach. I've no idea what I'm doing wrong.'

'Have you tried turning your phone off and on again?' Alistair said sarcastically.

'Yes,' Cameron said. 'It's made no difference. I'm technologically inept.'

Alistair chuckled, 'I just came in to tell you I'm off for the day.'

'Is it that time already?'

Cameron glanced at the clock. Sure enough it was only an hour until closing time.

'It is, and I'm picking Janet up in

twenty minutes so I can't hold on any longer.'

'OK Dad, thanks for coming in today and helping out.'

Cameron stood up to follow Alistair out onto the shop floor.

'No problem. Are you any closer to finding someone permanent?'

'I've someone coming in on Friday for an interview but I'm not holding out much hope. He signed off his last email with, *Thanks Dude, Love and peace* and ended with five kisses! We've never met.'

'Try and keep an open mind. You're probably not going to find another Emily.'

'Don't I know it!'

In the six months since Emily had left, Cameron had tried, and failed, to find a good replacement.

The longest anyone had stayed had been two months but one day the youth simply didn't turn up. Cameron had gone into a clothing store later that week to find him behind a till. He'd shrugged and said, 'The pay was rubbish, man.'

Cameron hadn't argued. The pay *was* rubbish.

Home To Home's sales were steadily improving and each quarter had seen a slight rise in profits, but that didn't mean he was flush with money. Any profit was still being ploughed back into purchasing new stock and he had to give himself some money to buy essential things like food and wood.

He was glad Emily had pushed him to sell his own woodworking products. Those items were selling as well as his main stock and creating them took his mind off his heartbreak.

He was still living with Alistair, who kindly wasn't complaining, but with Alistair's romance with Janet getting more serious by the week, Cameron knew it might become a problem soon.

Alistair left and the shop was empty so Cameron sat down behind the till and tried again with the photograph.

He'd taken it at the weekend when he'd gone to Logan Hall to meet up with Dottie and her daughter, Alice.

Dottie had phoned him to ask whether he and Emily would like to meet up with them there to witness the happy reunion of the two Dotties. Cameron had gone on his own and spent a happy hour in the company of the two elderly ladies.

He had been about to make his excuses and leave when something remarkable happened. Paul Standen turned up and the two women greeted him as if he was their long-lost best friend. It had been a lovely afternoon of remembrance and joy.

Cameron had taken a photograph of the two Dotties and Paul with Logan Hall in the background. He wanted to send the photo to Emily to show her what she had achieved. She would be proud.

He tried and failed with the photograph again.

'Why?' he muttered, 'Why, when they're on the same gadget, can't they meld together?'

He'd have to email Emily and ask her

how to do it. She'd sent him lots of emails with photo attachments from her travels, so he knew the problem with the attachments must be all him and his lack of tech savvy.

He scrolled through them now until he found one of his favourites — one where Emily was about to bungee jump off the Kawaru Bridge in New Zealand.

The view around her was stunning with its sheer cliffs and the azure river running far below, but that wasn't what made it one of his favourites. It was her smile. It was full of joy and exhilarated anticipation. She looked free.

He started to type an email to her . . .

Emily

As always I'm being an eejit when it comes to technology. How do I attach a photo to an email using my phone? I've no idea. I've considered stamping on the damned thing to see if that works! There must be a better solution.

I went to the Dottie meet up and didn't get a word in edgeways apart from when I was attempting to rebuff Farmer Dottie's flirting. She has a way with words that makes my toes curl!

Maddie has invited Dad, Janet and me to another one of her soirées. Do you think she'll bring out a load of eligible women for me? If so, what's your advice? And is the best place to hide in the downstairs cloakroom?

Cameron stopped typing. What to write now.

He'd written lots of emails to Emily that he'd never sent. Emails about being in love with her, emails asking her to come home right this instant, even one email where he'd suggested selling Home To Home and coming to America to be with her. They'd all ended up being deleted.

Instead he sent her cheerful emails about customers and anything crazy either of their parents were up to. He never touched on the serious stuff.

She sent him lots of emails in reply which were packed with details of the places she was visiting and the things she was experiencing. She was throwing herself into this trip with gusto. Gone was the Emily who never smiled. In every photo she sent him, she was beaming at the camera.

Nor was it lost on him that, in all her emails she never once referred to their kiss — or the fact that he'd asked her to come back to him.

In three days' time she was due to start her new job in America and every time he thought about it he felt a tiny bit sadder.

Cameron had promised himself he wouldn't pine for her. His father was right; it was time to settle down. He was determined he was going to date someone as soon as the right person came along. He definitely was.

So far nobody had.

His fingers hovered over the touch screen as he searched for something amusing to write.

The door to the shop chimed and a customer walked in. He was still staring at the phone but he could hear the person moving towards him so he put it down.

He'd finish the message later. Dealing with the customer would give him time to think about what else he could say.

He looked up and his normal words of greeting died on his tongue.

Emily was standing there.

Her hair was slightly longer and the skin on her nose and across her cheeks was softly golden and lightly dusted with freckles. She was smiling, shyly at him.

For once he had nothing to say.

'Hi,' she said. 'Alistair tells me there's an underpaid, overworked job going in your shop.'

He nodded, still unable to speak.

'Is it still available? Only I'm currently unemployed, you see.'

Cameron stood there gawking for

several moments before he finally moved around the till. He walked slowly towards her, afraid she was a figment of his imagination and that she would disappear at any moment.

He stopped when he was standing directly in front of her.

He cleared his throat.

'What happened to the American job?' he asked.

She took a step closer.

He could almost smell her; that light, fresh scent he often conjured in the middle of so many nights when he couldn't sleep.

He opened his arms and she stepped into them. His arms came around her and he pulled her tightly towards him. Her hands slid up his back and she buried her face in his chest.

'It wasn't for me. When I thought about working in a dry office environment instead of somewhere like here, I felt sick.'

His fingers tangled in her hair.

'So you've come back for this job?'

He felt her laugh against his chest.

Her hands came round to his front and she pushed herself away from him slightly so that she could look up into his face.

'And my desk,' she said softly. 'I really missed that.'

He lowered his mouth to hers and whispered, 'I love you,' and then kissed her.

She kissed him back.

★　★　★

Later, when Cameron had closed the shop early and they were sitting with a cup of tea in the storeroom, he finally dared to ask Emily if she was back for good.

'Yes,' she said definitively. 'I did a lot of soul searching at the beginning of my trip. I really thought about what direction I wanted my life to take and I realised that moving to America was just me trying to run away from reality.

'I'm going to set up my own web

design business, and find my own place to live in Brighton and . . . ' She looked at him intensely. A flush of pink was staining her neck. 'And I . . . well, I was wondering whether . . . '

'Your old job was still here?' he said, deliberately misunderstanding her.

She laughed and her shoulders relaxed.

'For the meantime I guess I can help you out for a bit but no, that's not what I was going to ask. I was wondering if perhaps . . . if you and I . . . '

Cameron took her hands in his, relishing the feel of her touch again.

'Emily, I would like nothing better than for us to be together . . . but what about Johnny?'

'I loved Johnny, with all my heart,' she said passionately. 'But if there's one thing I learned from Dottie, it's that there's more than enough room in my heart to love someone else too.'

She stood and Cameron stood too, taking her into his arms.

'It took me a long time to realise it,

Cameron, I love you, very much.'

'That's all I need to hear,' he said, wrapped her in his arms and kissed her once again.

MYSTERY AT MORWENNA BAY

Christina Garbutt

Budding criminologist Ellie is glad to help her gran recuperate after an accident, expecting to spend a quiet month in rural Wales before heading back to London to submit her PhD. But she's bemused to find that she's something of a celebrity in the village, and expected to help solve a series of devastating livestock thefts for which there is no shortage of suspects. She's also wrong-footed by the friendly overtures of handsome young farmer Tom — even though a relationship is absolutely the last thing she wants or needs . . .

JEMIMA'S NOBLEMAN

Anne Holman

1816: When her father's famous fan shop in the Strand is reduced to ashes, Jemima dons the clothing of a maid and moves with him to the docklands of London — and is present at an accident where William, Earl of Swanington, almost literally falls into her lap! But William is fleeing from accusations that he's murdered a servant — and when he sees the beautiful Jemima at a Society ball, he wonders if she's the one who robbed him after his accident! Can true love blossom in such circumstances?